Jane and the Kenilwood Occurrences

Jane and the Kenilwood Occurrences
by Frances Gapper

illustrated by Jill Bennett

FABER & FABER
London · Boston

First published in 1979
by Faber and Faber Limited
3 Queen Square London WC1
Printed in Great Britain by
Robert MacLehose & Company Limited
Printers to the University of Glasgow

All rights reserved

© *Frances Gapper 1979*
Illustrations © *Faber and Faber 1979*

British Library Cataloguing in Publication Data
Gapper, Frances
 Jane and the Kenilwood occurrences
 I. Title
823'.9'1J   PZ7.G/

ISBN 0-571-11359-1

To my Mother and Father
and my principal Literary Advisers,
John and Paul Gapper,
and to everyone in or connected with
the Cassel Hospital, Ham

Contents

1 Appearances   9
2 A Picnic and Peculiarities   26
3 Tea and Surprises   40
4 Disappearances   59
5 Changes   78
6 Strange Places   93
7 The Exact Opposite   107

CHAPTER ONE
Appearances

When Jane was nine years old, her mother and father both disappeared.

They had gone on safari in Africa for two weeks, leaving Jane behind in Kenilwood, but promising to send her a postcard every day. The first postcard was of a rhinoceros: on the back, it said "Hope you like this rhinoceros." The second was of a hotel: it said "Our hotel room marked with an 'X'. We had roast rhinoceros for breakfast." The third had a picture of a small aeroplane: it said "This afternoon, we are due to fly out over the desert." After that, there were no more postcards.

At the end of the two weeks, no one came home. After three weeks, Jane began to get a little worried. After four weeks, she decided to do something definite. When she came home from school on Friday afternoon, she climbed to the top of the house, opened what looked like a wardrobe door set into the wall, went up a spiral staircase into a very narrow passage-way, pushed up a trap-door directly above her head, and came out into a little attic with a table, a chair, a great many books and her grandfather in it. He was writing a History of the World, and every time he wrote a page he added it to a pile beside him. He had been writing for so long that the pile had risen far above his head, and loomed in an alarming manner, like an Abominable Snowman.

"Ah, Jane!" he said, after having looked at her for a long while as if he could not quite remember who she was. "I had a postcard from your mother about a month ago." He fished vaguely in his pocket. "Here it is. It has a picture of a rhinoceros on the front. She hopes I'm looking after you. Do you think I am?" he asked, anxiously.

"Not really," said Jane. "But I'm managing by myself. I go to supper with my friend, Maria," she added.

"Supper?" repeated her grandfather, in surprise. "Ah, yes, supper," he said, thoughtfully. "As you get older, you forget about these things."

"I came to ask for your advice," said Jane. Her grandfather suddenly became alert and attentive. He straightened up, leant forward, smoothed his hair, polished his glasses and put his pen down. "My dear Jane!" he said. "Of course, of course. What can I tell you?"

Jane explained. Her grandfather pondered. "I should wait," he said, after a while. "People often stay longer than they mean to. I've been on holiday from Russia since I was seventeen. I only meant to come here for a few days: now, I can't even remember how to speak Russian."

He picked up the page of writing in front of him, and stared at it. "Would you by any chance know anything about the Ancient Egyptians?"

"Not really," said Jane, sadly. "Except that they liked cats. I'd like a cat, too," she said. "Sometimes it gets a bit lonely, downstairs."

"My dear Jane!" he cried, again. "Of course, of course. I'll come down and visit you some time. What does the rest of the house look like, nowadays?" Suddenly, a tremendous clanging broke out. The window-pane trembled; the room shook; papers, books and ink fell off the table.

"Six o'clock," said Jane. "Maria will be expecting me for supper."

Her grandfather stared at the pool of ink. "It is useful to know the time, of course," he said, "but sometimes it gets a little irritating having a bell-tower right outside the window. Please come again!" he called after her, as she squeezed her way back down the passage. "Always glad to see relations!"

When Jane woke up in bed the next morning, she found that she was stuck. For a long time, she lay there wondering why, and finally raised her head and looked.

She was covered in cats. Fat cats, thin cats, striped cats, spotty cats, Persian cats and common cats: there was not an inch of blanket to be seen between them. And they were not only on the bed, but on the chairs, the floor, the mantelpiece, and even the window-sill. Most of them were asleep, but as soon as she looked up, fifty pairs of blue, green and yellow eyes opened, and switched towards her.

After a while, Jane slowly inched out from under the sheets, and sat up: immediately, all the cats began to mew and turn around. She made her way to the window, stroking as she went — it took a very long time. Meanwhile half the cats began to yowl, and a fight started up in the far corner.

Jane moved four cats carefully off the window-sill, opened the window, and looked out. Up and down the road, in the trees, on the cars, in every garden and on every wall, there was nothing to be seen but cats. In the middle of the road stood her friend Maria, with a small black kitten on her head, roaring with laughter.

"What's happened?" shouted Jane.

"Don't ask me!" cried Maria. "But isn't it funny?"

On the opposite side of the road, another window flew up, and Maria's mother leant out.

"Maria!" she shouted. "If you don't come in this moment, I shall get seriously annoyed. Jane," she added, spotting Jane, "stay exactly where you are. I am responsible for you, in your mother's absence."

"She couldn't move, anyway," said Maria, picking up a large ginger cat with white spots. "And neither can I: there are too many cats in the way. I'll just have to stay here, for the rest of my life."

"Don't talk nonsense, Maria," replied her mother. "If you got out there, you can get back."

Just then, two helicopters flew over, very low.

"They're scouting us out!" shouted Maria. "I wonder how long these cats go on for?"

"Four miles in every direction," cried her mother despairingly. "It's just come over the radio."

The helicopters flew back, even lower. A man with a loudspeaker leant out at a dangerous angle.

"Keep calm!" he boomed. "Keep very calm. Everything is under control."

"I'm glad to hear it," called Maria's mother irritably. "It doesn't look like that to me at all."

There was a sudden loud noise in Jane's room, and all the cats stopped mewing in surprise. Jane looked around, and up and down, but could see nothing. Finally, she realised it was her own stomach rumbling. "Breakfast!" she thought. All the cats looked at her, expectantly, and she realised she was not the only one who wanted breakfast. But where was there going to be enough to feed four miles of cats?

Across the road, an old lady who lived next door to Maria leant out of her window. She was holding a saucer full of milk.

"Kitty, kitty!" she called, extending it shakily in front of her. Two cats immediately leapt up onto her arm, and sank their noses into the saucer. "No, not you," she said, crossly. "Go away, do." But it was too late — the milk had disappeared and she was covered with a further wave of cats. "Oh Arnold, Arnold, where are you?" she cried. "Get off, you horrible things." And she shook them off, and slammed the window.

Meanwhile, in Jane's room, several cats were exploring the bookcase. Books showered down, and the radio came with them, switching itself on as it hit the floor.

"This is the Eight O'Clock News!" said the radio. "The cats who moved into Kenilwood early this morning have now begun to disperse. We have reports that several have already reached their homes, and those who live further afield are being helped on their way by a relay of helicopters. Some, who were travelling towards Kenilwood from places as far away as Cornwall and the Highlands of Scotland, have now turned back without reaching their destination. No one can offer any explanation..."

"Jane!" cried Maria. Jane rushed slowly to the window. The cats were moving. Most withdrew down the road in a slow procession. Others swarmed over the roof-tops and vanished beyond the chimney-pots. Gradually, Jane's room began to empty, and soon they had all gone.

Except for one. A very woolly white cat stayed under a tree, exactly where it was, washing itself. The old lady's window flew open.

"Arnold!" she cried, happily.

"I cannot understand it," said Maria's mother, for the fourth time. "I simply cannot understand it." And, also for the fourth time, Maria burst into giggles, and the sausage that had been in her mouth beforehand went all over the table. "Do try to control yourself, Maria!" said her mother, severely. "Go and get the dustpan and brush. And *do not* put that sausage back in your mouth again. Why can't you be like Jane, now?"

Jane, who hated sausages and had that moment put hers in her pocket, blushed and looked out of the window. Her eyes alighted on a most extraordinary person. On his head was a

14

sun-helmet, tipped over his eyes, and in one hand a parrot cage without a parrot in it. He was singing a very loud song about lions.

"Who," cried Maria's mother, "is that peculiar man?"

Jane looked harder. "It's my father!" she said, in astonishment. She ran outside.

"What are you doing?" she demanded. "Why are you singing that song?"

Her father stood still, and swayed. "Because if I don't," he said, "I shall fall asleep. Where's bed?"

"Just over the road," said Jane. She took hold of his elbow and pulled him back to their house. He collapsed just inside the front door.

Four hours later, he woke up, and Jane made him a cup of tea. "Bath," he said.

"Upstairs," said Jane.

He came back from his bath in a long red dressing-gown, with his hair plastered down all over his head. "Anything to eat?" he asked, hopefully.

"There's half a cold curry in the larder," said Jane. "Although it is a bit mouldy."

"What's curry without mould?" he replied. "On safari, we never ate anything else but mouldy curry. Lion curry, of course."

When he had finished the curry, he was rather red in the face. "Now we can talk," he said, sitting back.

"Where's Mother?" demanded Jane.

"Following," he said. "But I'm not quite sure when."

"What's she doing?"

"Catching parrots. Or, to be more accurate, one parrot. Our parrot. Or what was our parrot."

Parrots were going round and round in Jane's head. "I didn't know we had one," she said.

"We haven't. Your mother caught it on safari, and when we

15

got to England, the bottom of the cage dropped out. So we have no parrot."

Just then, a parrot flew in at the window. It settled on top of the refrigerator, and began pecking at the remains of the curry.

"That's a funny thing," said Jane's father.

"There have been a lot of funny things, lately," said Jane: and she told him about what had happened that morning. After she had finished, there was a pause: then —

"Nonsense, Jane," he said firmly. "Things like that simply do not happen. It's a good story," he said, waving his hand, "but you must never confuse truth with fantasy. I am now going to get dressed," he added, and went out of the room, avoiding the eye of the parrot.

Two minutes later, the door burst open.

"Cats!" exclaimed Jane's father. "Cats on my clothes! A chest-of-drawers full of cats! Curled up on my ties! Ruining my handkerchiefs! Scuffing up my shirts!"

Jane looked at him, crossly.

"I apologise!" he added hastily. "I was wrong and you were right. But please," he said, in a suddenly humble voice, "please get rid of them for me."

"Don't you like cats?"

"I can't bear cats!" His voice went up an octave. "They give me the shivers!" And indeed he was shivering — his hair had been shaken almost dry. The parrot was also beginning to shiver. Jane left them both in the kitchen, while she went upstairs to find out how many cats had been left behind.

Half-way up the stairs, she was hit at knee-level by a flood of cats, pouring over from the top. None of the cats had been left behind: they had all come back.

"Shut the door!" she shouted over the banisters. The kitchen door slammed shut, just in time, and a rush of cats pressed up against it. It would now be impossible for Jane to get back that way without most of them tumbling into the kitchen with her. So she sat on the top step, and thought.

All the way down the stairs and over the carpet she could see cats, winding backwards and forwards, in and out and round and round each other, in a kaleidoscope of fur. Only in one part of the hallway was everything entirely still. Entirely still. In front of the door, twenty or so grey cats, smooth and enormous, sat bolt upright. Their faces came to a point at the nose and went out to a triangle at the ears. They had very heavy lids to their eyes. And they sat absolutely quiet, with their tails curled over their feet, not looking at each other, nor at anything else. Jane felt rather glad that they were so far away: she also felt that she had rather not go any closer to them than was necessary.

Jane's house was the oldest in the street, and interesting in many ways, especially because there was generally more than one means of getting from place to place. There were, for instance, two routes into the kitchen: one through the ordinary door, and one through a trap-door under the bath.

A few minutes later, Jane landed on the kitchen table, beside her father.

"It's very dark in here!" she said, surprised.

"I have closed the curtains," said her father, with dignity. "I prefer not to look outside."

Jane switched the light on. "Don't be silly," she said, feeling superior. Her father glared at her.

"You're getting very bossy, Jane." He looked most strange, still in his red dressing-gown, with his hair and moustache unbrushed and sticking up, and the parrot on his shoulder. "You should behave with respect to your parents."

"I do respect you really," said Jane kindly, trying not to laugh.

Suddenly, everything seemed to go very quiet. Jane drew back the curtains and looked out into the street. It was empty, except for Arnold.

"I am not moving one step out of this kitchen," announced Jane's father. Jane opened the door, and looked into the passage. There was not a cat to be seen. "They'll be back," said her father, darkly. "Mark my words, they'll be back. Shut the door!" he ordered, huddling together with the parrot. Jane shut the door, and turned on the radio.

". . . And the cats have once more retreated," said the radio. "They do not appear to have done any damage. It is as yet undecided . . ." Here, the voice suddenly broke off, and resumed in a deeper tone. "Warning — warning! A small number of these cats may be extremely dangerous — Repeat, dangerous! They can be identified by their pointed faces, heavy eyelids and particularly long tails. They appear to have come to England on an Egyptian trading vessel . . ."

"You see?" cried her father. "Not that those cats could possibly have managed to get as far as this," he added, dubiously. Jane thought it would be best not to tell him about the twenty silent cats she had seen in the hall. But she went and checked the kitchen door again, to make sure it was firmly closed.

After two hours of waiting around doing nothing, Jane began to get impatient.

"I'm going to see Maria." At that very moment, a loud cry came from the street. Jane pulled open the curtains again. Maria was standing on the opposite pavement, surrounded by large, grey cats with pointed faces. Jane recognised them immediately. She threw up the window, and began to climb out.

It took her a long time to get to Maria, pushing through the sea of cats, slowly and heavily, as if she were walking in a dream. Even before she got there, the Egyptian cats had disappeared. They turned in stately procession and moved away up the road: and the other cats made way for them.

"I feel strange and woozy," said Maria, staggering into her

house. "Those pointed faces made me go all shuddery inside. What I need," she said, "is lots and lots of brandy."

"You need nothing of the sort, Maria," said her mother, "but you can have some Strengthening Glucose, if you like. What were those dreadful grey creatures?"

They were just having a tablespoon of Glucose all round in the front room when Jane looked out at the street again, and her heart leapt into her mouth.

The street was emptying quickly: but as fast as the ordinary cats vanished, their places were filled. Now there were not just a few of the strange Egyptian cats, but hundreds, pouring in, grey and menacing. They flowed up onto the walls, into the trees, over the roofs, settled quietly down and waited.

Jane started to feel very strange: not ill, but cold and tired. It seemed as if she sat there for hours, staring at the floor and thinking of nothing, before she remembered the open window that she had left behind her: would her father have closed it again in time? How was he feeling now, with all those hundreds of grey cats waiting outside, when even ordinary cats frightened him so much?

Jane hardly knew how she got to the front door and out into the street. She kept her eyes fixed on the sky. It was a very bright blue, and the sun was blazing down, but in spite of that it was so cold that Jane's legs could hardly move at all. She knew that she must be pushing her way through cats, but where the other cats had been solid and warm, these were light and feathery. Her feet were numb, and as she walked the numbness gradually spread upwards to her knees. By the time she had reached the middle of the road, she could not even feel her legs any longer. She stood still, swaying. Then she began to sink down.

Without looking, she could sense hundreds of bright yellow eyes. There was a curious smell in the air, like a very old and musty perfume, and the nearer she got to the ground, the stronger it became. The light, feathery touches moved round her arms and her shoulders.

Then she felt two hands under her, and she was on her feet again.

"I've walked all the way from Southampton," said her mother, smiling cheerfully. "Following a parrot. A very pleasant journey. This seems to have been declared a danger zone," she added. "No buses or trains: such a nuisance."

"The cats..." said Jane.

"Yes, indeed." Her mother aimed a kick at the nearest one, but missed. They had withdrawn to a distance, leaving a wide space of pavement clear. "As a rule, I like cats," she said. "But I can make exceptions."

Jane stamped her feet, to test them. The numbness had disappeared, leaving only a tingling feeling.

"I leave this country for four weeks," said her mother,

resignedly. "Four weeks. And look what happens. Things get quite out of hand. Where is your father? And how did all this business start? No, don't answer," she continued. "Before anything else, I must go inside and tidy up."

Inside the house, Jane's father was lying on the floor by the kitchen table with his eyes shut. The parrot was nowhere to be seen.

"Do get up, Alfred," said Jane's mother, shocked. She propped him up against the kitchen table. He opened and shut his mouth once or twice, and shivered.

"Why are you both so blue and frozen?" said her mother. "Jane, explain."

Jane explained. After she had finished, there was a long pause. Then her mother walked thoughtfully up and down the room a few times, looking at the floor. Then she came to a halt, and waved her fingers in the air.

"It would seem that we have here three problems," she announced. "Number one: why are these new cats not going in and out, as you say the other ones did? Number two: why does everyone else get so weak and floppy, but not me? Number three: why did it all start happening in the first place? Excuse me."

She put a hand up to her head and pulled out the scarf tied around it.

"I must comb these beetles out, they're so tickly. The ship sailed through a cloud of Red Egyptian Beetles," she explained, "and most of them seem to have stayed with me." As she combed, little taps on the floor announced that the beetles were falling.

"I get all my best ideas when I'm combing. Rather sweet, aren't they?" she said, looking wistfully at the beetles waving their legs.

"Aha!" she exclaimed after a while, shaking the comb as if it had caught an idea. "Problem One solved. The cats don't go in and out to get food because they're not hungry. Most cats need food, but, for some reason, not these."

"Ho, hum," said Jane's father, with a rude yawn.

Jane opened the curtains and looked out. Hundreds of cats looked back at her. She switched the curtains into place.

"There are *more* of them!" she whispered. "And they're all staring at this house!"

Her mother dropped the comb and began stamping her feet, avoiding the beetles. "My feet have gone dead," she said. "How strange."

"It's still so cold," said Jane's father. He closed his eyes. Jane's head turned funny and she sat down at the table. The beetles stopped waving their legs.

"Keep awake!" ordered her mother, stamping harder. "Keep awake and listen to me! Nothing happened to me until now, and I think it was because of my beetles. They came from Egypt, like the cats. That must tell us something. The cats are all looking at this house — that must tell us something else. Egypt and this house . . . Heavens above! Is there a lemon sorbet in the larder?"

"Pardon?" said Jane, yawning.

"A lemon sorbet. Something very like this happened about twenty years ago, and, as I remember, a lemon sorbet cured it immediately. Where is my recipe book? Where are the lemons? Jane, run up and down and keep your blood going round!"

Jane ran. Her father was slumped once more on the floor. "We must be the only people awake in Kenilwood," she thought doubtfully, as she passed backwards and forwards, "and we're making lemon sorbet. Shouldn't we be fetching help?" But she kept her thoughts to herself, and in a very short time the lemon sorbet was produced.

"Upwards!" cried her mother, holding the sorbet aloft. "We have someone else in this house, although your father has forgotten it."

"I know," said Jane. "I visit him sometimes."

In four minutes, they emerged into Jane's grandfather's room, dusty and breathless.

"My dear Amaryllis!" he said, pushing his glasses back. "My dear Jane! How nice!" He got shakily to his feet, and the toppling pile of papers finally crashed to the ground.

"Father!" cried Jane's mother. "Stop thinking!"

"Stop thinking?" he repeated, in a reproachful tone. "It's my duty to think. I'm writing a very important History of the World."

"At this moment," said Jane's mother, "it is your duty to stop thinking. Take a look out of the window."

"Oh, dear, dear," he muttered, having looked. Jane ran to the window herself. The cats were thick on the sloping roof beneath and clustered on top of the bell-tower. Their eyes flashed at her, malevolently.

"You have been thinking far too much about Ancient Egypt," announced Jane's mother. "With the results that you see below."

"I was thinking about cats for Jane as well," he said, mournfully. "My Egyptian thoughts would seem to have got mixed up with my Cat thoughts."

"Well, now you must stop thinking."

"It's easy to say, my dear Amaryllis. I cannot stop thinking just like that."

Jane's mother waved the lemon sorbet in front of him, smiling smugly.

"Well, bless my soul! A lemon sorbet! It must be at least twenty years..."

"Mother!" cried Jane, from the window. All the cats below had closed their eyes.

"Shush!"

"A lemon sorbet with bits of lemon on the top!" continued her grandfather, with relish. "Would there be a spoon to go

23

with it?" Jane's mother produced a teaspoon from an inner pocket, and handed it over. "Take it slowly," she said. "Don't think about anything else. I knew it would work," she added, under her breath.

"The cats!" cried Jane. "The cats are fading!"

"Hmm?" said her grandfather, momentarily distracted from the sorbet.

"No — now they're coming back!"

"*Do* be quiet, Jane!" hissed her mother, despairingly. "Let your grandfather attend to his sorbet."

"Now they're fading again," said Jane — but she said it to herself. Not only could she see the roof-top between the cats, but she could see it through them. They were disappearing like smoke. By the time her grandfather's spoon scraped on the bottom of the dish, there was nothing left of them but a little dust, which blew off into the air.

"Delicious!" announced her grandfather, downing the last traces, and putting his hand up to shield a polite burp. "There's nothing to match these good old secret family recipes. Well, I must be getting on. The Peloponnesian War comes next, and I see all sorts of fascinating possibilities in it."

"Just so long as they don't come to Kenilwood," said her mother sternly.

"Of course not, of course not. Don't hustle me, Amaryllis. You know I don't make mistakes like that more than once every decade or so. Once cured, seldom recurrent. Like the measles. Well, goodbye," he added. "Not to hurry you, but time rushes on."

"I have never met anyone so rude as your grandfather," said Jane's mother wonderingly, as they squeezed back down the corridor. "You would think he'd be glad to see his only daughter, especially as I haven't been to visit him for six months."

"I think he was glad," said Jane. "It was just difficult to see, because of his beard. Will you teach me the ancient family recipe for lemon sorbet?"

"Ancient family recipe, my foot," replied her mother. "I got it out of *Woman's Own*. Everything is all right!" she cried, as they entered the kitchen. "All men can get up off the floor, all parrots can come out from inside the breadbin."

"As you can see," said Jane's father, in an injured tone, "I am no longer on the floor, but standing quite respectably on the table. Opening the window to air the room," he explained.

"You can blame it all on Father!" continued Jane's mother, exuberantly.

"I beg your pardon?"

"Not on you, dear, on my father."

"What?" he said. "Don't tell me the old man's still in the house! I thought he'd gone back to Russia, or up to happier places."

"Yes, he is, but I'm not telling you where. You'd only start shouting at each other again. At our wedding," she told Jane, "your father leant over the table and pinched Grandfather's cake-icing, which he had been saving on the side of his plate until last. And Grandfather then insisted on taking your father's slice, to make up. They've never forgiven each other."

"It was all his fault!" cried Jane's father, beginning to shout. But Jane was not there to hear him. She had gone up to the top of the house, through the wardrobe door, up the spiral staircase, along the very narrow passage, and was helping her grandfather to sort out his papers. She felt he needed keeping an eye on.

CHAPTER TWO
A Picnic and Peculiarities

When Jane was nine and a half years old, her grandfather took a holiday from his History of the World, and they went picnicking in the park.

"Mother," she announced, "Grandfather and I are going picnicking. In the park."

"Good," said her mother. "A bit of fresh air up his nostrils will do him no harm at all. What sandwiches would you like?"

"Honey, please," said Jane. "And ham with lettuce. And peanut butter, crunchy. And jam-and-banana. And Grandfather..." she said, handing over an envelope.

"What is this funny envelope?"

"I think," replied Jane cautiously, "it's what Grandfather wants in his sandwiches."

Her mother broke open the envelope and took out a tiny, folded piece of paper. "Definitely not!" she cried. "He can have sausage-and-salad-cream, and put up with it."

Jane's grandfather appeared in the doorway. "I am ready to depart," he said, in a dignified manner. "And if I cannot have lemon sorbet in my sandwiches, I shall have nothing at all. Anything else will be fed to the ducks."

"Quaark!" said Jane's father, pretending to be a dying duck.

Her grandfather peered at him over his sun-glasses. "What," he said, nastily, "is that horrible fluff on your chin?"

"It's a beard!"

"Well, it's dreadful. No shape."

"What about yours, then? It just goes on and on. On and on and on and on and..."

"Alfred!" interrupted Jane's mother severely.

"As you please," said Jane's father, putting on a haughty expression. "I shall retire to my room, to write my History. *I* haven't got time to waste going picnicking."

"What History?" cried Jane's grandfather.

Her father gave him a nasty stare. "I just happen to have started writing a History of the World," he replied. "Any objections?"

Jane's grandfather was speechless.

"Honey," said her mother, handing her a carrier-bag. "And ham with lettuce. And peanut butter, smooth because we've run out of crunchy. And jam-and-banana. And," she added, raising her voice, "sausage-and-salad-cream!"

"I shall go," said Jane's grandfather, going. "And I hope your beard blows off!" he hissed backwards at her father.

Jane's grandfather spluttered all the way to the park. "Him and his so-called History!" he fumed. "And him and his silly whiskery bits! Him and his ... Good Heavens!" he exclaimed, stopping to peer at a woolly thing leaning against a tree.

"A dog," said Jane.

"Of course," said her grandfather, looking more closely. "A dog. Rather like a cat ... only different."

"Well!" thought Jane to herself. "If he can't even recognise a dog, it *is* time he went out for a walk."

"It has a label around its neck," went on her grandfather, pushing up his sun-glasses. "The label says ... Alexei! That's my name! How can a dog have the same name as me? And on the other side," he said, turning it over, "it says ... 'Airam'."

"'Airam?'" repeated Jane.

27

"Hiya!" said Maria, appearing from behind the tree with an American accent. " 'Airam' is a secret code, so that nobody knows whose dog he is. Maria, spelt backwards. I called him Alexei because he has extra-long fur, just like you, Mr. Bostov, only all over."

"Very funny," said Jane's grandfather, coldly.

"He's a peculiar sort of dog," said Maria. "He drinks practically nothing but Strengthening Glucose. I've had to start eating his Good Dog Choc Drops. Come on, Alexei, pick up your toes, we're going to catch a fish this afternoon, if it kills us."

"Where would he catch a fish?" said Jane's grandfather, walking after her. Jane was just in time to stop him before his feet went into the lake. Over the water came loud barks and despairing whistles, as Maria tried to explain to Alexei what a fish looked like. Jane's grandfather lay on his back and filled his ears with grass. "I shall lie in the sun," he said, "and think of various things."

Jane went to help Maria, and stayed on the other side of the lake until evening. When they finally came back, without any fish, her grandfather was still on the ground. His nose had turned pink.

"Where are the ham sandwiches?" cried Maria. "Where are the peanut butter, and honey and jam-and-banana sandwiches?"

"All the sandwiches," replied Jane's grandfather, "are inside me. I got used to them after a little effort. I found the jam-and-banana very stimulating to the thoughts. It brought me a most interesting idea."

Jane and Maria looked at each other. "Not *too* interesting, I hope," said Jane.

"That's as may be," he said, mysteriously.

"Clang!" went something in the distance, and they all peered into the dusk and wondered what it was. Maria thought it might be the warning bell for Closing-time, which would leave them half an hour to spare. But there were no more clangs, and eventually they realised it had been the park gates actually closing.

"Well, blow me down," said Jane's grandfather. Just then, a cold breeze actually began to blow. Jane's grandfather pulled his collar up, and his hat down, and they ran for the gates. The first star appeared in the west. "I cannot stop thinking," shouted Jane's grandfather, "of that very interesting idea that came to me."

"I wish you would stop thinking," said Jane. "Something might..."

It was too late. Strange things were already happening. The wind was beginning to blow very hard. Jane's grandfather's hat and Maria's hat both spun off across the grass. The wind began to swirl around them like a hurricane, and the air became suddenly as thick as rice pudding with falling blossom.

For every one step forward, the wind blew them two steps back. Their legs ached and their feet slipped, and soon they found themselves at the lakeside again. Even then, the wind went on, forcing them into the water. Jane felt it splashing up around her legs, biting cold. Still the wind continued, and she was blown further and further in. Just before the water reached her waist, Maria grabbed one of her arms, and her grandfather grabbed the other, and she was hauled up into a large rowing boat. The boat, tied to a tree at the side of the lake, was already scissoring back and forth, straining at its moorings: just as Jane fell in, the rope snapped and they shot out into darkness.

The shore disappeared behind them as the boat skimmed over the water, and blossom stung their faces, and the wind roared around them. Jane put her head down in her lap, with her hands around it, and felt Alexei's ears flapping against her. She thought of the headlines in the newspaper the next day: "Children, Dog and Old Man Shipwrecked and Drowned in Kenilwood Boating Lake." It sounded so silly that she would have laughed if she had not been sure that it was going to happen any moment. Then, suddenly, the wind dropped, the moon went behind a cloud, and they were in absolute darkness and silence. The boat slid on for a few more yards, crashed into something solid and stopped.

Jane's grandfather sat up in the bottom of the boat and coughed out some blossom. The moon appeared from behind its cloud, and shone down on his beard. There was much, much less of it.

Jane was beginning to understand. She remembered her father leaning out of the window and shouting about beards blowing off; she remembered her grandfather looking at the falling blossom; and she remembered his Interesting Thought.

"Grandfather!" she said. "Were you thinking about Father's beard?"

"I apologise," said her grandfather, sheepishly. "But all the same," he said, "it would have been so nice if your father had been here and if his beard *had* blown off."

"Well, it serves you right," said Jane, "that it was your beard that went thin, instead."

"What?" he cried, looking at his beard for the first time. "Oh, no!"

Meanwhile, Maria was examining Alexei. "This dog looks different, somehow," she said. "Much more handsome and distinguished. Good grief!" she cried. "All that extra-woolly hair over his eyes has disappeared! He can see! Mr. Bostov," she said, beaming at Jane's grandfather, "you're a clever man."

Meanwhile, the blossom still fell. "Has anybody got the oars?" said Jane.

Nobody had. The boat had been blown out with no oars, and now they were helpless.

"Could you think of a tiny bit more wind?" asked Maria. "Just a small breeze, to get us back to shore."

30

"My thoughts never seem to work as well, on water," said Jane's grandfather.

Jane suddenly realised what a narrow escape they had just had. If the boating lake had not been there, her grandfather's thought might have gone on and on; the wind might never have died down; and the whole of Kenilwood might have been blown away entirely. At that moment, Alexei put his head into the water to have a drink and fell out of the boat.

"Hold on, Alexei!" shouted Maria, falling out after him. "I'm not sinking!" she called back. "Why not? I'm standing on a platform! There's an arm on my shoulder — I'm sitting on someone's lap!"

Jane leant out of the boat and saw: Alexei's face, looking excited, Maria's face, looking surprised, and a large white face, looking very calm.

"We must have reached the middle of the lake," she said. "You're sitting on the statue."

"So I am!" said Maria, standing up. "Hiya!" she added, shaking hands with the statue. The hand came off. "Well, I expect it was getting pretty old, anyway," she said, hooking it onto the other hand.

"Excuse me, Jane," said her grandfather, climbing past. "I feel somewhat safer out here," he explained, joining Maria on the statue. The boat sank even lower. Jane got out as well. The boat sank altogether.

Maria sat on the statue's lap, Alexei sat on Maria's lap, Jane's grandfather held onto the stone snake that the statue was brandishing and Jane held onto him. Alexei looked at the sky, and howled.

"Exactly how I feel," agreed Maria. "OWWOOooo!" she added, joining in. Jane's grandfather fell backwards in surprise, and disappeared from sight. After a while, his voice came up from behind and beneath, echoing strangely.

31

"I'm somewhere else," he said. "Underneath. How comfortable it is."

"He's fallen through a sort of hole!" cried Maria, leaning over. "He's in a little room under the statue!"

Alexei came suddenly up through her legs to have a look, slipped with his front paws, and disappeared too.

"Woof!" he said, as he went.

"Woof!" said Jane's grandfather, as Alexei landed on him.

"Watch out!" cried Maria, as her feet slipped after them. Jane waited until they had all become untangled and then let herself carefully down by the hands.

They were in a round, dark cave, like the inside of a teapot. Light came in through the small hole above them, and through it blossom fell, and beyond that the stars shone very clearly. Alexei sniffed around to make sure that everything was safe, and found a mop and a bucket. "This must be where the Park Keeper keeps all the things to clean the statue," said Maria. A sound of snoring came from inside the bucket. Alexei had put his head in, and gone off to sleep.

"I hope," thought Jane to herself, crossing her fingers, "that nothing else will happen, now."

Her grandfather was peering up through the hole. "A most odd and amazing thing is happening," he said.

"Oh, dear," thought Jane.

Very high up, higher than the moon, higher than most of the stars, a tiny needle-point of light was moving: and as it moved, it got rapidly larger and larger.

"A meteorite!" said Jane. "It's coming towards us!"

"Don't worry," replied her grandfather, with assurance. "There is only a million-to-one chance of its coming to earth."

The point became yet larger.

"And if it did come to earth" he added, after a while, "there would be another million-to-one chance of its actually hitting England."

A few moments later, the point of light had become very large indeed.

"Well, if it did hit England," he said, "it would almost certainly not come down in this park."

The point turned black, and became an enormous boulder, spinning down from the sky. "Although I may possibly be mistaken," said her grandfather. It hit the shore with such force that the whole statue rocked and shuddered. A vast mushroom cloud of blossom shot up into the air. Alexei remained completely asleep.

"A very interesting phenomenon," said Jane's grandfather, polishing his sun-glasses.

"I wonder," thought Jane to herself, "whether it could possibly have started falling towards us at about the same time as Grandfather started thinking?"

"Grandfather," she said, aloud, "do you suppose that the same thoughts that brought the blossom down..."

"We must go and examine it," interrupted her grandfather. He yawned. "In the morning."

In the morning, Jane found herself lying under a blanket of blossom, with the sun shining through the hole onto her face. A quavery, faint voice floated down to her.

"Hullo?" it said. "Is anybody there?"

Jane threw off the blossom and went out. The voice belonged to a very bent, white-haired old lady, carrying a basketful of bread.

"Do you always sleep in the statue?" she asked. "And where have all my birds flown to?"

Jane was not quite sure how to answer either of the questions, so she put the old lady off with a question of her own.

"How did you get here?" she said.

"I walked."

Jane looked out across the lake, and saw to her surprise that the water had vanished. It was blocked solid with leaves and blossom. Anyone might walk across it, like a carpet. Far away, where it met the grass, all the rowing boats were beached high and dry.

"I don't know what the Park Keeper's going to say about this," said the old lady doubtfully.

"I don't know, either," said someone else, coming round from behind the statue. "And I am the Park Keeper. I just cannot think of a word to say."

Scuffles and muffled woofs came from inside the statue. The others were waking up.

"There was a very strong wind, last night," observed Jane, by way of making conversation. "I don't need to say why there was a very strong wind," she thought to herself.

"But why was there a very strong wind?" said the Park Keeper. "There was nothing of the kind anywhere else. All the rest of Kenilwood was perfectly peaceful."

"I slept like a bird," agreed the old lady. "But where did all the birds sleep? And where are they now?"

"Perhaps if you started throwing your bread, Madam," suggested the Park Keeper, "they would be attracted. Cleaning out the pond," he muttered, "will be rather more of a problem than usual this year."

The old lady threw a handful of bread onto the blossom. In three seconds, Alexei was out of the statue and had gobbled up the lot.

Maria came up behind him. "Alexei!" she shouted angrily. "Go home!" Alexei trotted off guiltily in the direction of the park gates.

The next handful of bread was very successful. A cloud of swans, geese and ducks appeared out of a clear blue sky and clattered down. But they had no sooner eaten the bread than they looked around them in bewilderment and vanished again.

"There's nowhere for them to swim," said the old lady,

getting sad and worried. She threw another handful. More birds appeared, and again dispersed.

"I shall employ all the schoolchildren," announced the Park Keeper. "Instead of doing paper rounds, they can come and take the blossom away in buckets."

"But what will the birds do till then?" cried the old lady, clasping her bag of bread.

Jane's grandfather shaded his eyes from the sun, and peered at her. "You sound very like someone I used to know," he said. "Good heavens, Miss Smith! You were twelve years old when I first came over from Russia, and you gave me a loaf of bread. I see you are still being just as generous. Perhaps I could have a crust for breakfast this morning?"

"Mr. Bostov!" cried the old lady. "I thought you had gone back to Russia. Are you still writing that History of the World? I remember that, in 1918, you had just come to the Ancient Egyptians. Certainly — have two crusts."

"This is all a dreadful muddle," complained the Park Keeper. "Here are yet three more people, and the gates not even officially open. And that dog is back, as well."

Jane's mother and father and Maria's mother were waving by the boats. They all had red scarves on, and Jane's father had a balaclava helmet. In a three-minute run, they were at the statue. Jane's mother hugged Maria, and Maria's mother hugged Jane. Jane's father got a camera out from under his coat, and began taking pictures. "I'm a reporter now," he said. "I'm on the staff of the *Kenilwood Herald*. What a scoop, for my first day on the job. It almost makes up for the beard disappointment."

"The beard disappointment?" repeated Jane's grandfather, nervously.

"Yes," said Jane's father, "most of my beard strangely fell out last night. Hullo, yours has got thinner too. Well, that makes me feel much better."

Jane's mother finished hugging Maria, and hugged Jane: and then she hugged the Park Keeper, for good measure. "What a fine time those ducks are having," she said.

"Ducks?" said the old lady, eagerly. "My ducks?"

"Over on the other duckpond," said Jane's mother.

"What duckpond?" said the Park Keeper, the old lady, Jane's grandfather, Maria and Jane.

"Back the way we came," said Jane's mother.

"I will escort you, Miss Smith," offered Jane's grandfather, and they went off together, with the Park Keeper running ahead.

"Most extraordinary," went on her mother. "A whole new duckpond seems to have been created, just as if a vast Something had fallen suddenly out of the sky and made a big pit for the lake to fill up with water. The birds are enjoying themselves no end."

"We must get back home," said Jane's father. "I have to send my report in before the *Kenilwood Star* and the *Kenilwood Eagle* and the *Kenilwood News-sheet* come around with their cameras as well."

"Back home," said Maria. "I have to give Alexei his breakfast."

"Back home," thought Jane. "I hope I won't have to make up too many explanations."

"I will not ask for any explanations," said her mother. "I know that when your grandfather is on form, fairly unexplainable things are always liable to happen."

When Jane and her mother and father got home, they found it was time to have lunch. Then, a little later on, they had supper. Then, just before they were about to go to bed, they realised they had never had breakfast.

"This is a good excuse," said her mother, "to have an extra meal. An eleven o'clock at night Celebration Meal, for everyone being safe, your father getting a good story for his newspaper and your grandfather finding a friend. We'll have a guest, and boiled eggs."

So she rang up the Park Keeper, and he came round at once, very pleased. "Eleven o'clock Celebration Meals," he said, "are the only ones I can ever come to. I'm always too busy looking after the park for anything else." He brought a bottle of wine, to drink with the boiled eggs.

"One egg left over," announced Jane's mother, at the end of the meal. She put a purple egg-cosy over it, and told Jane to hand it in to her grandfather on her way up to bed. "Tell him it will make his beard grow," she advised.

Jane's grandfather was sitting up in bed with a nightcap on, knitting. There was a duck on the inside window-sill. When it saw the egg, it gave a muffled but indignant squawk, and flew away.

"Take that egg down to the kitchen again," ordered her grandfather, without looking up.

"I think you ought to eat it," said Jane anxiously. "It would help your beard to grow."

"I make beards grow my own way," he said, looking secretive, and continuing to click away with his needles.

"Don't be silly," said Jane. "You can't knit yourself a beard."

"Just watch me."

"Actually," admitted Jane, after watching for a while, "it's not a bad beard at all."

"Stocking-stitch."

"Who taught you?"

"Someone. Well," he said, casting off and putting his needles under the pillow, "time to be quiet."

"Goodnight," said Jane. "I didn't know you ever had time to sleep."

"I do not," he replied, haughtily. "I simply lie in the darkness, and think intelligent thoughts about my History of the World."

Jane took the egg through the trap-door, down the ladder and along the narrow passage-way. Even before she stepped out into the main part of the house, she heard him snoring.

CHAPTER THREE
Tea and Surprises

One Wednesday morning, when Jane was nine and three-quarters, ten letters came through the door. All but three of them were for Jane, and most of them were knobbly.

"Another gas bill," groaned her father.

"Another library fine," sighed her mother.

"Another letter from the Society for the Preservation of Ancient Monuments," complained her grandfather, when she took his letter up to him. "What have you got?" he demanded suspiciously.

"Seven free samples," said Jane happily: and she lined them up along his mantelpiece. Two plastic soldiers, one packet of needles, some sugar for slimmers, some pills to put on weight, a tiny envelope of dried fruit juice, and a pencil sharpener. Downstairs, the letter-box gave another little click.

"Something else?" demanded her grandfather eagerly, when she came back with the late letter.

"Yes," said Jane, handing it over. "No stamp — someone must have delivered it by hand."

"Just as I thought," he said, unfolding it with a smug look on his face. Three pressed flowers fell out onto the desk. The notepaper was pink, with a pattern of roses. "How nice," said Jane's grandfather, reading it. "I am invited to tea."

"Who's invited you?" asked Jane curiously.

"So nice, to be invited to tea."

"Yes," said Jane. "Who's invited you?"

"I shall wear my hat," he went on. "And my long coat, with silver buttons."

"You'll look good," said Jane. "Who's invited you?"

"You do ask a lot of questions," he said, huffily.

"I'm asking the same question, a lot of times," pointed out Jane.

"A lady has invited me," he said. "She also invites me to bring a guest, or possibly two. So you may accompany me — and that strange friend of yours. Friday, at four o'clock."

Jane went to tell Maria that she was invited. "Sorry," said Maria. "Friday's my day for not having tea with people. But you can take Alexei, if you like. He enjoys being asked out."

Jane was rather doubtful as to whether Alexei was quite the right kind of dog to take out to a tea party, so she said nothing, hoping Maria would forget. However, at three o'clock on Friday, Alexei was sitting outside her front door with his tail combed and a bow around his neck. He looked most odd, but very respectable. Jane's grandfather descended the stairs, looking equally out-of-the-ordinary.

"I hope that dog doesn't think he's coming with us."

"No, I'm sure he doesn't," said Jane, feeling very guilty. "Shoo, Alexei!" she added, under her breath. Alexei stayed exactly where he was.

"On second thoughts," said her grandfather, "we might be able to incorporate him into our plans. Do you think he likes rock cakes?"

Alexei put on the face of a dog who likes rock cakes very much indeed.

"Because, if he did," went on her grandfather, "he could sit under the table and eat mine. I'm almost sure we'll have them, and I dislike them extremely."

So all three of them set off up the road together, feeling

refined and well-dressed. Half-way along, they met a cat, coming in the other direction. When Alexei came back, he was his old untidy self again, with an extra nick in one ear.

"Really!" said Jane's grandfather, crossly. "That dog is a disgrace. He looks dreadful."

At that moment, he himself walked straight into an approaching tree, and came out of it looking just as dreadful. Jane tried to improve things by brushing them both up and taking leaves out, but one of her grandfather's buttons was missing, and it ruined the whole effect.

"Never mind," he said. "A free-sample button might have arrived by the time we get there."

"A what?"

"A free-sample button. I was inspired by all those interesting things on my mantelpiece. Your mother lent me the stamps. By my calculations," he said, "I should be due for a silver button, a small packet of soap powder, an indoor firework and a plastic soldier. They would all have arrived by the last post."

"Shall we go back and get them, then?" said Jane.

"We'll go forward and get them," he replied. "I knew better than to send off our address. Your father would have laughed. And here we are!"

They were in front of a small, dilapidated house. It had a hedge outside, with four ducks on it. Jane began to suspect whom they might be visiting.

When they got to the door, Jane rang the bell, but it was broken. Then she tried to use the knocker, but it had rusted up. Then Alexei barked, and the door opened. It was the old lady who had been so worried about the birds at the lake.

"You've brought a dog," she said, looking pleased.

"Yes, indeed," said Jane's grandfather. "A very well-behaved dog. And my granddaughter. And also . . ." he added, producing a hyacinth from underneath his coat, "a hyacinth.

It hasn't come out yet, but when it does, it will be white."

"White," said the old lady, "is my favourite colour."

"What a coincidence! "cried Jane's grandfather. "It's my favourite colour, too."

"I've always liked white."

"I, too."

At this point they were interrupted by Alexei, who put his head up in the air, laid his ears back, and gave a tremendous yawn.

"A very rude dog," said Jane's grandfather coldly. "I apologise for him."

"Not at all," said the old lady, "I know some ducks who are just as rude. Come inside. I'll just go and get a needle and thread."

She stepped back, and disappeared completely. "Go straight through to the kitchen!" she cried, from somewhere in the depths. Jane looked doubtfully into the darkness. Alexei went straight through. Jane remembered just in time that tea would probably be set out on the kitchen table, and flew after him to make sure he went under the table, not onto it.

"What's for tea?" asked her grandfather, hurrying anxiously in.

"Rock cakes."

"Ah," he said, sadly. "Ah!" he cried, more cheerfully, spotting the table. "I see my place has been set." He sat down and began to unwrap a pile of little envelopes arranged round his teacup.

The old lady came in again, with her needle and thread. "I saw you having difficulties with that tree from my window," she said, looking rather nervous. "So I took the liberty of quickly unwrapping your free-sample button. Let me sew it on for you."

"I wouldn't dream of it!" cried Jane's grandfather. But the old lady was already sewing it. "I cannot thank you enough," he said, as she cut the thread. "No one knows how to sew buttons on, nowadays."

The kettle whistled on the stove. Jane stepped backwards, to let the old lady pass, and her foot went through a rotten floorboard. She pulled it out again, and pretended nothing had happened.

"Have a rock cake," said the old lady, pouring out the tea. Jane's grandfather took a cake, and passed it straight under the table to Alexei, who swallowed it in one gulp. The old lady handed Jane her tea first, and almost dropped Jane's grandfather's

cup when she saw how quickly the cake had gone. "Have another," she offered, looking surprised and delighted. "I'm so glad they came out nicely. They have egg glaze on top."

Jane's grandfather, very ashamed, took another rock cake. She looked the other way, to pour out her own tea. Jane's

44

grandfather cut the cake in half, spread a little margarine on it, and devoured it in four bites. "Delicious," he said.

"Delicious," agreed Jane, who had already eaten two, with jam. Alexei laid his head on her grandfather's lap, with an injured expression.

"I see my plastic soldier never came," said Jane's grandfather, who had now unwrapped all his envelopes. "But what are plastic soldiers," he went on, gallantly, "when one is having tea in a beautiful house, with a charming lady at the teapot."

The old lady blushed. Jane took another rock cake, and wondered how he could possibly think the house was beautiful. It was very clean, but there were no curtains or carpets and the only furniture in the room was the table and three stools.

By the end of tea, the stars were beginning to shine through the window. "I would turn on the light," said the old lady regretfully, "but it doesn't seem to turn on, these days." She stuck a little candle in the sugar bowl, and lit it. Jane's grandfather took out his free indoor firework, and lit that, too. It spurted blue and green for five seconds, while Alexei grabbed the last rock cake.

"Come again!" cried the old lady, waving goodbye to them at the door, and throwing the rock cake crumbs to the ducks, who had gone to sleep on the hedge. "Come next Wednesday!"

"I never noticed it before," said her grandfather, when the house had disappeared in the darkness, "but I think Miss Smith may not have very much money."

"Neither have you," said Jane.

"She has no curtains," went on her grandfather. "She has no carpet. She has no ginger biscuits."

"She has birds," pointed out Jane.

"True," said her grandfather. "But then, what are birds? They take your crumbs, and fly away."

"She has a house," said Jane.

"A few poky rooms and a corridor," said her grandfather. "Very dark and gloomy."

"She has you," said Jane, hesitantly.

"Absolutely!" cried her grandfather, with enthusiasm. "And she will have a great deal more of me from now on. I am determined to make things easier and more comfortable for her."

"We could ask her to tea," suggested Jane.

"No," said her grandfather. "Definitely not. I cannot make rock cakes, and your father might alarm her. So we will go to tea with her. But we will make matters better for her. We will help her in all sorts of little ways. For one thing," he said sternly, "we will take no more dogs."

Next Wednesday, at four o'clock, Jane and her grandfather set off again. Alexei was waiting outside the front door, with a friend. They both had bows around their necks. "Go away, dogs!" cried Jane's grandfather. Jane could have told him it was no good. The dogs walked up the road with them, one on each side. After a little while, two more dogs joined them, also with bows.

"This cannot go on," announced Jane's grandfather, standing stock-still in the middle of the pavement. "Under no circumstances can I take more than one dog to a tea party. Preferably none at all."

"I don't think there's much we can do about it," said Jane.

"The chocolates," replied her grandfather, "will have to be sacrificed." He took a box of chocolates which they had just spent all afternoon wrapping in red paper, and threw them over the roof-tops, in a beautiful spin. Three dogs immediately vanished. Alexei remained.

"Now we've nothing to give her," thought Jane sadly.

"Fortunately," said her grandfather, "there are certain other things which she may have received by now. Four things, in fact. Your mother would only lend me four more stamps," he explained.

There were five ducks and a swan on the hedge outside.

"Come in!" cried the old lady, opening the door. The swan at once leapt off the hedge and waddled inside. "Please excuse the swan," she added, "he has a wife and four babies to visit in the bathroom. Step carefully," she went on, as they followed the swan, "the hallway is rather crowded. A lot of travel catalogues arrived this morning."

"Good heavens!" exclaimed Jane's grandfather, who had just tripped over one pile of them and fallen onto another. "I only sent off for one. These travel firms are far too enthusiastic. Fond though I am of Transylvania," he said, "I would not wish to visit it seventy times in one summer."

"Do sit down," offered the old lady. Jane's grandfather sat down, in his usual place.

"What's this!" he cried, seeing three envelopes round his cup. "These are not meant for me. They're for you."

"For me?"

"All for you," said Jane's grandfather, generously. "Every single one."

The old lady could hardly believe her ears. "What a lovely packet of almonds," she said, unwrapping them. "What a lovely plastic soldier. And two carpet samples — I can use them as table-mats."

"I only wish there was more," said Jane's grandfather. "But one comes to the end of one's stamps."

"Yes, indeed," she agreed. "I came to the end of mine six years ago. Have some tea. Have a jam sandwich. I also came to the end of the currants for the rock cakes," she added, looking apologetic. "I hope you don't mind."

Jane's grandfather did not answer at all. He was staring into the middle distance with blank eyes. Jane passed her hand in front of his face.

"Ah!" he said, coming to. He took a jam sandwich, crumbled it in an absent-minded manner into his cup, and stirred briskly.

47

"Grandfather!" hissed Jane. The old lady pretended not to notice. Jane's grandfather looked at the soggy mixture in surprise and poured it into his saucer for Alexei, who gulped it. Then they started again, and both Alexei and Jane's grandfather behaved quite respectably for the rest of the meal.

"I remembered yesterday," said the old lady, hesitantly, "that it's my birthday tomorrow. I am seventy-two."

"A child! A child!" cried Jane's grandfather, waving his latest jam sandwich in a nonchalant way.

"So I would be very much obliged," she went on, even more hesitantly, "if you would come to tea again."

"Delighted," said Jane's grandfather. "Yes, please," echoed Jane, wondering what there would be for tea, as she could see nothing in the cupboard at all. And the old lady had saved her own sandwich: as they waved goodbye at the gate, Jane turned round to see her taking it out of her pocket and dividing it into neat pieces for the ducks.

Jane's grandfather was somewhere else all the way home. His feet walked in the right places most of the time, but Jane had to direct him round corners. She hoped he was not thinking too hard, but she was practically sure he was.

When she met him at the front door the next afternoon, his eyes were still glazed and distant. "You haven't brought a present," she said. She herself had a very long melon-seed necklace, done up in a piece of tissue paper, which it had taken her considerable trouble to make. She had been saving seeds from every lunch-time melon for the past eight weeks, and then she had put them in the bathroom basin to soak the bits of melon off, and her father had gone into the bathroom to shave and had let the whole collection down the plug-hole. He told Jane it was her fault, and that no sensible person would ever want to make a melon-seed necklace, anyway. Jane thought he ought to buy her some more melons, to make up. He said he would do no such thing, and went back down to his study to continue with his History of the World. Jane's mother, who was good at settling quarrels when she was not quarrelling herself, rang up the greengrocer and ordered four more melons.

"Your father won't see the bill for at least a month," she said, reassuringly. "And by that time, we will have eaten all the evidence." And Jane had stayed up all night making the second necklace.

Her grandfather, however, did not appear to have anything at all. "Never mind," he said mysteriously. "Certain things may have arrived by the time we get there."

"I thought you had run out of stamps."

"They may still have arrived."

On the hedge outside the old lady's house were four ducks, a swan and a bald-headed coot. The old lady herself took a long time to get the door open.

"Come in!" she said, breathlessly. Her arms were piled high with envelopes. "Ah!" said Jane's grandfather, with satisfaction.

"Shut your eyes before you go into the kitchen," she said, in a squeaky, excited voice. "You'll never guess what."

Jane guessed what without even opening her eyes. It was soft and squashy under her feet. "A carpet!" she cried.

"A free-sample carpet," agreed the old lady, proudly. Jane opened her eyes, and blinked them several times. The carpet was dazzling. It was in about forty-seven different colours.

"A whole carpet as a free sample?" she said.

"In instalments," explained the old lady. "Bits at a time. I've been fitting them together all morning. And I think," she added, putting her armful of envelopes down in the corner, "that another mat's worth has just arrived."

"Well, well," said Jane's grandfather, smugly. "Let's all sit down and have tea. Ah! Baked Almond Slices — my favourite."

"Yes," said the old lady, "a great many packets of almonds

have been coming, as well. I just cannot understand about all these free samples. Especially as we have run out of stamps."

"I can," thought Jane to herself.

Jane's grandfather took a satisfied bite of Baked Almond Slice. "What a very charming blue hyacinth," he said, changing the subject and coughing as a crumb went down the wrong way.

"You gave it to me," said the old lady. "It just turned out blue," she added apologetically. "Blue is my second favourite colour."

"Is it, now?" Jane's grandfather leant back to digest. "It is also my second favourite colour."

"I've always liked blue."

"I, too." There was a sudden clatter, as of things hitting the front door mat. The old lady disappeared down the corridor.

"Perhaps," said Jane, "you should stop thinking now."

"Stop thinking?" repeated her grandfather, innocently.

"Yes," said Jane.

"I admit," said her grandfather, trying without success to look modest, "that my thoughts may have something to do with all this. All is well, however. What has obviously happened is that the addressing machines at two free-sample factories, under my influence, have stuck at the same address, and are simply repeating it on envelope after envelope. That's why nothing is coming but almonds and bits of carpet, again and again. It will only be a matter of time before someone realises what is going on, and adjusts them to normal once more. It may even have been done already."

The old lady re-entered the room, with her arms overflowing. "Most odd," she announced breathlessly. "No envelopes at all. Simply things. Things by themselves." She piled them onto the table. "Bars of soap," she said, sorting through. "Two candles and a box of matches. Iced buns. Tea bags. A tin of Good Dog Choc Drops. A bottle of Strengthening Glucose. A china duck. A banana. I haven't had a banana," she cried, "for years."

"Is it still you?" whispered Jane, while the old lady was putting the tea bags into the pot, and opening the tin of Good Dog Choc Drops for Alexei.

"I suppose it must be," whispered back her grandfather. "My subconscious is working without envelopes."

"It was very clever of you to think of the banana," said Jane admiringly.

"I didn't think of it on purpose," he explained. "If I had been thinking on purpose," he added stiffly, "I would certainly not have included the Good Dog Choc Drops. No dog around here deserves them."

There was another sudden loud clatter at the front door.

"Four more bars of soap," said the old lady, coming back in. "Pink, yellow, green and rainbow-coloured. Two packets of soup, leek-and-tomato and bean-and-broccoli. A guide to the London Railways. And," she went on, unrolling an enormous roll of paper, "three maps of Italy, showing where the wines, cheeses and sheep are. How beautiful," she said, looking at them admiringly. "And they'll cover those damp patches on the wall. Let me just find the drawing-pins . . . oh dear, I have no drawing-pins."

There was yet another click at the letter-box. Alexei trotted off to find out what it was, and came back with a small red box in his mouth. "Good gracious, a packet of drawing-pins!" cried the old lady.

Jane's grandfather held the posters in position, while she pinned them up and hung the china duck between them. Jane suddenly remembered the melon-seed necklace: the old lady had to wind it round three times because there were so many seeds. When she had finished winding, she was crying.

"My dear Miss Smith!" exclaimed Jane's grandfather, leaping to his feet. "Allow me," he said, producing a faded,

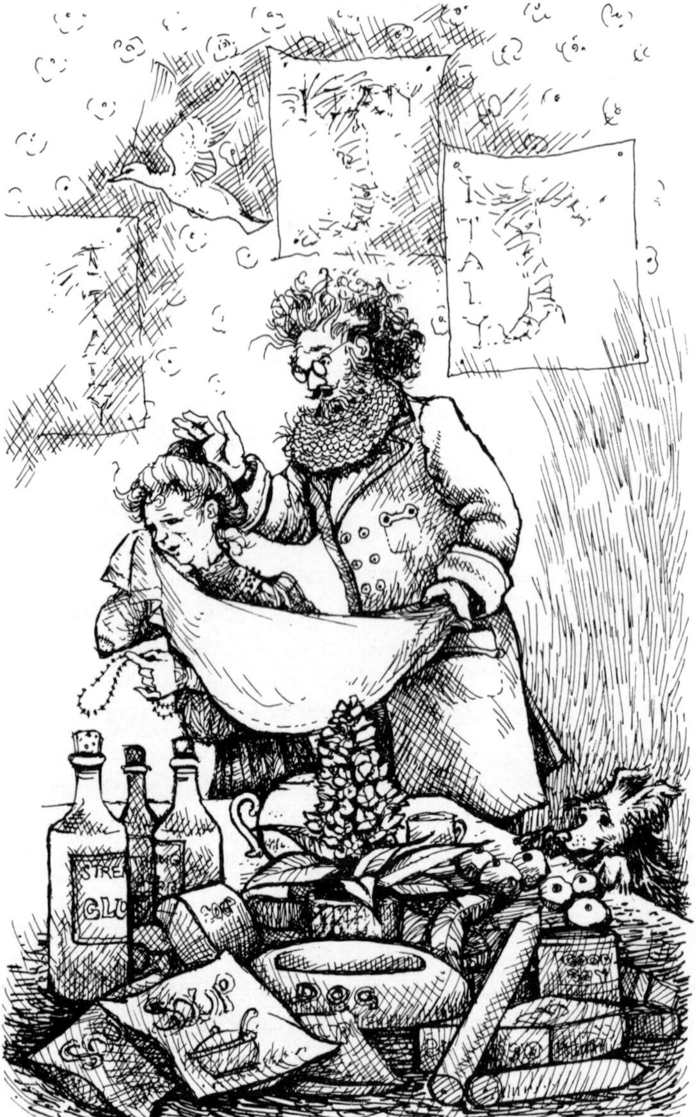
I T A L Y
SOUP
DOG

lemon-coloured handkerchief, which was so large that while she was wiping her eyes with one corner, the other corner was still in his pocket.

"It's so long," she sobbed, "since I've had any presents at all. And now I have people to tea, and things to give them for tea, and melon-seed necklaces, and bananas, and oh, it's all so nice!" she said, with another burst of tears.

The letter-box rattled again, and Jane went to answer it. She had to come back for a candle, to light up the hall. There were three white handkerchiefs, embroidered with the initials "A.S.", and done up in a gift box. There were, in addition, four bottles of Strengthening Glucose, a Collapsible Dog-bowl and a packet of bird seed. There was a pocket dictionary and a book on ducks. Jane picked up as much as she could and returned to the kitchen. The letter-box went on clicking.

Her grandfather was pacing up and down in the kitchen, looking at the ceiling. "I am fascinated," he said, "by that trap-door. Miss Smith says she has never actually opened it."

"We have lots of trap-doors at home," pointed out Jane.

"This is an unexplored trap-door," said her grandfather. "Who knows what might lie behind it?" He got up on a chair and pushed, but nothing happened. He pushed harder, but still nothing happened. Then he pulled a little ring, and immediately fell to the floor beneath a pouring deluge of packets of soup, nuts and margarine, books and handerchiefs, pencils and balls of wool and wrapping-paper and tulip bulbs. "Hum," he said, sitting up in the middle of the pile. "Things would also appear to be coming through the roof."

"It is time," said Jane, firmly, "that you stopped thinking."

"Stopped thinking?" repeated the old lady. Jane's grandfather looked at Jane, and Jane looked at her grandfather. "This may be a little difficult to explain," he said.

"I'll tell you what it sounds like," said the old lady, looking rather surprised. "It sounds like something I was once told by my brother. He used to come to tea with me," she said, sadly, "but he doesn't seem to any more. Well, he said that someone that both of us had once known, when I was very young, had thoughts that sometimes made things actually happen."

"Me!" cried Jane's grandfather, in astonishment. "Who is this brother of yours?"

Suddenly, someone's voice came through the letter-box and floated down the hall. "Alexandra!" it shouted. "Are you there? I've come to tea!"

The old lady hurried down to open the door. "Good heavens, Pompous!" she said.

"It just struck me," said her brother, stepping inside and falling over various heaps of things, "that I had not been to tea with you for twenty years. So here I am."

"I have other visitors, too," answered the old lady. "Although I am glad to see you, of course."

"Pompous!" cried Jane's grandfather, from the end of the corridor.

"Alexei Ivanovitch Bostov, my dear man!" They rushed into each other's arms and banged each other on the back.

At last, the old lady's brother disentangled himself. "Tell me, Alexei," he said, "are you still Thinking?"

"To a certain extent," said Jane's grandfather, cautiously.

"Useful things?"

"Of course." Jane's grandfather waved his hand proudly at the heap underneath the trap-door.

"My dear man!" cried the old lady's brother, again. "We can make millions! All this can be sold. More, I believe, is arriving," he added, hearing the letter-box click. "That can also be sold."

"Will you have a cup of tea, Pompous?" asked the old lady timidly.

"Later, Alexandra, later. Yes, indeed," he continued. "Keep it up, my dear Alexei."

"Well," said the old lady, even more timidly, "I think we have enough, now."

"You don't see the *point*, Alexandra. There can never be enough of anything. Profits are to be made. Soon you will be able to move to a bigger house. I will move with you. You will be able to travel round the world."

"What for?"

"You will have new summer dresses and warm winter boots," he went on, ignoring her. "You could even have a fur coat."

"I like this dress," she objected. "And I still have Mother's boots. And I would never, ever wear a fur coat."

"Well, mohair, then."

"Certainly not!" she cried, indignantly. "Poor little Mo."

"Persuade her, Alexei," appealed her brother, turning to Jane's grandfather in despair.

"I would never try to persuade Miss Smith," he replied, "of anything she did not want to be persuaded of."

The old lady's brother slurped crossly at his cup of tea. All this while, the letter-box had been clattering and things had been falling from the trap-door. A bunch of plastic roses landed on his feet, and he gave them a peevish kick.

"Neither of you have any sense of business," he said. "You will not get on in this world."

"I've got on very well indeed for eighty-seven years," replied Jane's grandfather haughtily.

"Yes, and look at you! Thin as a rail. No books published."

"Look at you," retorted Jane's grandfather, with spirit. "Fat. My History of the World," he went on, "will be published just as soon as I finish it. I have, what is more, a very good friend, who invites me to tea. I have a daughter, a granddaughter, a friend of a granddaughter, and a friend of a granddaughter's dog. And, finally, my beard is longer than yours."

"Part of it is knitted," accused the old lady's brother, peering at it closely.

"Yes, and I can knit!"

A duck quacked outside the window. "Aha!" said the old lady's brother, holding his finger up. "You like birds, don't you, Alexandra? Well, if we started selling, you could have an enormous aviary, to keep them safe in."

"Oh, dear," said the old lady, dithering and wringing her hands. "But perhaps they wouldn't like it much, anyway."

"It's your own decision," he said, picking up an almond slice and looking at her out of the corner of his eye.

"Oh dear, oh dear!" cried the old lady.

"Pompous!" said Jane's grandfather. "You are despicable. Look how you are upsetting your sister."

"She has no sense of realities," said her brother, finishing the almond slice. "She will end up poverty-stricken in the gutter!"

"I should like to say something . . ." announced Jane's grandfather.

"Well, what is it?"

There was a pause. "I should like to ask Miss Smith," said Jane's grandfather, "if she would do me the honour of becoming my wife."

Miss Smith's brother choked on his second Baked Almond Slice. Jane dropped the Strengthening Glucose bottle. Alexei stopped drinking. There was absolute silence. Even the letter-box was quiet.

"Miss Smith," said Jane's grandfather, "will you marry me?"

"I will!" she replied, with decision. She took off her apron, and hung it over the top of her chair. Then, not knowing quite what to do next, she poured out an extra cup of tea for everybody. Jane's grandfather sipped his, and beamed.

Miss Smith's brother found his voice again. "Impossible!" he declared. "Neither of you knows what you're doing. Also, I am her only surviving relative, and I have not given my consent."

"You are not my only surviving relative," retorted Miss

Smith. "We have a sister in the country. And besides, I am over twenty-one, and I can do what I like."

Her brother took the last Baked Almond Slice, and bit angrily into it. "Well," he said, another idea occurring to him, "you will now need money more than ever. I very much advise you to fall in with my plans."

"Too late!" announced Jane's grandfather, triumphantly. "Nothing is coming through the letter-box. Nothing is dropping from the trap-door. Enough has arrived, and there will be no more."

"You've stopped thinking!" cried Jane and the old lady, together.

"I have stopped thinking," he agreed. "Or, rather, I am thinking of you, Miss Smith, for you are more important than anything else."

"Soppy," muttered her brother. "I will not be coming to the wedding," he added, heaving himself out of his chair. "I am going now, probably for good." And he slammed the door behind him.

"What a terrible temper Pompous has," said the old lady, disapprovingly, "How glad I am that I only see him once every twenty years."

For the last half-hour, they sat round the table together and made arrangements. Jane wanted the two of them to get married immediately, so that she could be a bridesmaid, but they both turned out to believe in long engagements. "I am not irresponsible," declared Jane's grandfather, "whatever your brother may think. We must save money."

"Quite right," said the old lady. "And I must learn how to keep house for two. I will go to my married sister in the country for a few months, to be taught how."

"And I will finish my History of the World," said Jane's grandfather. "Or at least," he amended, "I will finish the Ancient Egyptians."

It was now too dark for them to see each other's faces. The old lady gave them a candle each, to light them home.

When they got back, Jane's mother met them at the door. "You," she cried accusingly, pointing at Jane's grandfather, "have been Thinking!"

Jane's grandfather jumped, guiltily.

"The bathroom is infested!" she said. "There are terrible weeds, twining up the plug-hole and round the taps. Alfred is in his study, having a nervous headache."

"Oh, no!" said Jane. "The melon seeds! They're growing!"

Her mother was silent for a long time. "Well, Father," she said finally, "I apologise."

"I should think so!" answered Jane's grandfather, drawing himself up haughtily.

"Of course," went on her mother, "you gave up Thinking — Thinking with a capital 'T', that is — months ago."

"Never mind," said Jane's grandfather, looking slightly uncomfortable. "We all make mistakes." Something roused itself from his shoulder, shook its wings and flapped heavily off down the corridor.

"What's that?" cried Jane's mother.

"Just a duck," he said. "They come and go," he added vaguely, going as well.

"Your grandfather seems to have changed a great deal lately," said her mother, peering after him. "I wonder if I ought to consult the doctor about him?"

"I shouldn't worry," said Jane. "I think he'll be all right."

CHAPTER FOUR
Disappearances

Jane woke up one morning at half-past four, with the birds calling to each other in the trees and the sky just beginning to turn pink. She lay quite still and wondered why she was not sleeping.

After a while, she realised that it was because she was worrying about something.

And that something was her grandfather. For the whole of the past week, he had kept to his room, with the trap-door locked and bolted, answering no calls, taking in no food and ignoring his post, even the free samples.

Jane's mother had been listening through the crack in the trap-door. "I can hear him going up and down," she reported to Jane. "Pace, pace, pace, Thump. Pace, pace, pace, pace, Thump. Anyone who didn't know him," she said, "would think he was tidying his room."

And soon the pacings and the thumpings had become so loud that everyone in the house could hear them quite easily. "Pace, pace, pace, thump. Pace, pace — Thump."

"It's like African drums," said her mother. Jane started walking in time to the beat. Her father found himself writing his History of the World in rhymed verse, and was quite pleased. Soon, they had simply stopped thinking about it and gone on as usual.

But now Jane, lying in bed, at half-past four, with the sky turning pink, suddenly realised that a change had occurred. The pacing had stopped.

At the very same moment she realised it, she also noticed something else: a glorious smell. It was so lovely that she leant over the side of the bed to see if roses could possibly be growing up through the floor — but the carpet looked much as usual. She breathed in deeply, and the rose smell went right through her, to her toes. Meanwhile, the sun appeared through the gap in the opposite houses.

Jane lay back on the pillows and wondered if anyone else was awake. Just then, there was a crash below, like a chair going over.

"Burglars!" said Jane to herself. She crept very softly out of the room and downstairs, taking great care to avoid the creaky floorboards. Then along the corridor, step by step, very slowly. Gently, she pushed open the kitchen door.

It was not a burglar: it was her mother, walking round and round the kitchen. "Peace," she said, sniffing as she walked. "Blue Moon. Golden Showers. But it was something else that woke me up," she decided.

"No pacing?" suggested Jane.

"No pacing!" cried her mother. "That's it!" She came to a halt. "We will have a half-past four in the morning cup of tea, to celebrate. And your grandfather shall come to it. No," she corrected herself, "on second thoughts, as his legs might be slightly worn out, perhaps we had better take it up to him."

Jane held the three cups of tea, one on top of the other, while her mother knocked at the trap-door. No answer. Then her mother took the three cups of tea, while Jane knocked. Still no answer. Finally, her mother drank the first cup, because it was getting cool, and Jane drank the second cup, to keep her company. Then they both knocked again. They were just about to divide the third cup between them, when her mother knocked extra hard, and the trap-door lifted up.

The room was absolutely empty. It was also extremely tidy. All Jane's grandfather's papers were laid out in large, neat piles along the wall, his chair was underneath the desk and his pencils were arranged in a little jam-jar. The smell of roses was stronger than ever.

While Jane and her mother were still staring, the door-bell rang downstairs. They rattled down with the empty cups, and her mother undid all the catches and latches and locks and flung it wide.

There was nobody there.

"Is it usually as exciting as this at half-past four in the morning?" demanded her mother. "I must get up early more often. This kitchen is a disgrace," she went on, as they entered the kitchen. "It makes me feel all fidgety. I refuse to be outdone by your grandfather. I shall have a half-past four clean-up. First of all the breadbin," she announced, shaking out the parrot. "This loaf of bread will have to go. No time to make it into crumbs — the birds can do the hard work." She opened the window and threw out the loaf entire. It fell straight into the mouth of a large dog waiting beneath.

The dog turned out to be Alexei. "Hiya!" said Maria.

"Everyone seems to be awake," thought Jane.

"Why didn't you answer the front door?" continued Maria. "Alexei got impatient, so we came round the side. Alexei has problems," she said. "He can't sleep."

"He'll have more problems soon," retorted Jane's mother. "Being sick problems."

"Not Alexei," said Maria, proudly. "He has an iron stomach. No, it's his head that hurts. He's worrying, because his ball has disappeared."

"I'm worrying," said Jane, "because my grandfather has disappeared."

"Alexei is very fond of his ball," went on Maria.

"And I'm very fond of my grandfather," thought Jane.

"So I'm organising a search-party," said Maria. "As early as possible, before any other dogs find it. Everyone else has been very unreasonable. My mother won't come, and nor will my father."

"And nor will I," added Jane's mother. "And nor, I should think, will Alfred."

"But if you came, Jane," said Maria, cajolingly, "we might come across your grandfather on the way."

Jane found herself walking along the road towards the park with Maria. Alexei was sick in the gutter, but looked very cheerful afterwards.

It was perfectly quiet, except for the sound of birds. The sun had risen above the roof-tops, and the last wisps of pink were dissolving in the sky. "What a lovely smell," said Maria. "Duke of Windsor. Dorothy Wheatcroft. Fragrant Cloud."

"I can't smell anything," said Jane. She sniffed, and found that her nose was blocked.

"Have my handkerchief," offered Maria, kindly. "It took me all the sewing lessons this term to embroider it," she added.

The initials in the corner were "S.A."

"Seraphina Andrews," explained Maria.

"I thought your name was Maria."

"Yes, but I like a change now and again."

Jane blew her nose thoroughly, and immediately smelt roses. "Thank you," she said.

"Don't mention it," said Maria. "Seraphina Andrews is a very good handkerchief. Could I have her back, now?"

But Seraphina Andrews had disappeared.

"I dropped it," said Jane. They looked round and about and up and down, but the handkerchief was nowhere to be seen. Maria lay on her stomach and peered down a drain. "Everything I lose," she said, "pocket-money in particular, always goes down drains. The worst was last week — Mama told me to collect her wedding ring from the jewellers, and I gave it to Alexei on the way back, to see if he could carry small things without swallowing them. Of course, the stupid dog had to cough directly over the only drain in the street."

"Wasn't your mother upset?" said Jane.

"She doesn't know yet," sighed Maria. "I'm still trying to remember what street it was."

Jane lay down on her stomach as well — but all they could see was their faces staring up at them, reflected in the drain water. Suddenly, there was another face as well. Jane and Maria sat up. It was Miss Smith's brother, Pompous, in a running suit, with his beard in a plait. He was holding a large bag.

"Good morning, Mr. Smith," said Jane.

"You may call me Mr. Smyrnovitch," he said, with dignity. "If you sit in the gutter, little girls, you will become dusty."

Jane began guiltily to brush her jumper down, but found to her surprise that she was quite clean.

"Moreover," he went on, "you will get bits of litter in your hair."

Jane looked across at Maria's hair, but there was no litter at all. However, she did not quite like to contradict him, so she said nothing.

"Well," he said briskly, "I can't stand here chatting all day. The big race begins soon. I must get to my starting mark." And he heaved his bag over his shoulder, and jogged off.

Maria was lying on her back, gazing at the sky. "Something is peculiar," she said.

"I think it's Mr. Smyrnovitch," said Jane, gazing after him.

"No, said Maria, vaguely. "Something else. Something to do with the road and the gutters and the drain and the pavements and the walls and the bottoms of the trees and the sky. I'll think of it in a moment."

Alexei took advantage of her thinking to lie down on top of her. "In a way," remarked Maria, "I'm sorry I put on my Sunday dress today. Dirt underneath and dog hairs on top — it doesn't matter to me but Mama gets edgy."

Alexei spotted a cat on a wall, and suddenly disappeared. Maria sat up, gasping. "That dreadful push he gives with his back paws," she said, hoarsely.

"Maria!" cried Jane. "I've just realised what it is! Everything's absolutely clean!"

Maria looked down at herself. "No dog hairs," she said. "No dirt."

"No litter under the trees," agreed Jane. "No leaves in the gutters."

"And no clouds," said Maria, lying back again. The sky was now blazing blue and empty.

Footsteps echoed along the road. "There's that funny man again," observed Maria. "That Smyrnovitch person."

"The paper chase is on!" cried Miss Smith's brother, rushing by. His bag was open, and he was throwing handfuls of paper behind him as he ran. There was no one else in sight.

"I went on a paper chase once," said Maria. "It was quite fun. You follow the bits of paper, to catch the person who's running ahead, throwing them. The only boring part is, picking all the paper up afterwards."

Jane watched him disappearing into the distance. "I think this paper chase will be different from most," she said. "It'll be a lot harder for the people following."

As each handful of paper floated to the ground, it faded gently away, like a shower of snowflakes. "Now we know," said Maria, "what happened to Seraphina Andrews. And Alexei's ball."

"He'll go on and on running all morning," said Jane. "No one will ever catch him, because they won't know where he is."

"Here they come!" cried Maria. "The Kenilwood Running Club!"

The Kenilwood Running Club rounded the bend, running hard. Some of them were scanning the ground for pieces of paper, but most had given up the effort and were simply following the rapidly vanishing figure of Mr. Smyrnovitch.

"Silly old men!" said Maria.

"Shush, Maria!" said Jane. But all the Kenilwood Running Club had white beards, and they did look rather silly. "Both my great-uncles are in that lot," said Maria.

"You never told me you had any great-uncles."

"I keep them as quiet as possible," said Maria. "You can see why. There they are, the fattest and floppiest, running behind all the rest."

Mr. Smyrnovitch had now vanished altogether, and the Kenilwood Running Club were beginning to look desperate. They slowed down, and finally stopped.

"I think we ought to find Mr. Smyrnovitch," said Jane. "If he went on and on until he had a heart attack, it would be all our fault."

"It would be nothing to do with us," said Maria, staring at her.

"Yes, it would," said Jane, conscientiously. "Because we didn't tell him in time that his paper was disappearing." She did not add another disturbing thought that had just come into her mind: that it was quite possible her grandfather might be at the back of the disappearances.

"Come on then!" cried Maria, leaping up. In a few minutes, they had left the Kenilwood Running Club far behind.

As they ran, people were beginning to come out of their houses and set off for work. Most of them had slightly puzzled looks on their faces, as if they were trying to work out what was different about the town. Some had obviously dropped things already, and were searching the surrounding pavement in bewilderment. Doors were opening and closing, and front-door mats were being shaken and looked under.

"Hasn't the milk been, this morning?" demanded a man with a fierce, bristly moustache.

"I did think I might get a letter, today," sighed his neighbour.

"Where are the newspapers?" said someone else, coming out in a pink dressing-gown.

"Oh, dear," thought Jane to herself, running by.

Maria got the giggles, and had to stop and gasp. But by that time, they were almost out of Kenilwood and at the foot of a very steep hill. Mr. Smyrnovitch had still not come into sight.

"This is a strange hill," said Maria. "Whenever people come down it, they always seem to be carrying enormous suitcases. I've always wondered what happens at the top. Sometimes Alexei decides to go and see, but he generally gives up before he starts. Come on, Alexei, today's the day."

Alexei sat very firmly down in the middle of the road and began searching himself for fleas. It was obvious that today was not the day. So Jane and Maria set out to climb the hill by themselves.

"We should have brought a packed lunch," said Maria, half-way up. "And a bottle of lemonade." They were both red in the face and sweating. Maria pulled her jumper over her head. "Watch out!" warned Jane. It was too late. The jumper had already fallen to the ground and disappeared. Jane took hers off as well, and tied it carefully round her waist: but a few steps later, the knot came loose and the jumper was gone.

Three-quarters of the way up, they sat down to rest. The whole of Kenilwood was spread out beneath them in the sun, gleaming bright. Jane, remembering something she had once read about the air being stronger in high places, took a deep breath; but the only thing that was stronger was the smell of roses.

"Look at all those tiny little people," said Maria. "Going

backwards and forwards and round and round. Everyone wondering where everything is. That must be the Kenilwood Running Club, outside the pub."

Jane looked, blinked and rubbed her eyes. The sun was certainly getting very fierce, for all the houses, walls and roads in Kenilwood seemed to be merging into each other.

"My eyes have turned funny," said Maria, rubbing hers as well. "What's happening down there?"

"Everything's going white," said Jane. "Absolutely everything, except the grass and the trees and the people." She looked at the road they were sitting on. "Even up here."

All the town was dazzlingly, blindingly white, as if it had been newly washed over with bleach. The trees looked greener against it, and the people looked blacker.

"It's only in Kenilwood," obseved Maria. "Look — there's Bagworth out beyond, as nice and grey and dusty as it always has been. Peculiar things," she said, reflectively, "only ever seem to happen to Kenilwood. Jane, I think this is something to do with your grandfather."

"I'm sure it is," said Jane, gloomily.

"Shall we go down again and search for him?"

"We're nearly at the top," said Jane. "Let's just find out what happens there."

The sun got hotter as they climbed, and the sky got bluer, and the road shone whitely up at them. "I wish we'd brought Alexei," said Jane. "He could have pulled us along."

"Not a chance," said Maria. "We'd have been pulling him."

"I wish we'd brought some lemonade," said Jane.

"I wished that before," said Maria.

"I wish we were at the top," said Jane.

"We are," said Maria.

At the top of the hill was a post, and on the top of the post a notice saying "Green Line Coach Stop". Underneath the post was a large, old-fashioned pump, and beside the pump was a

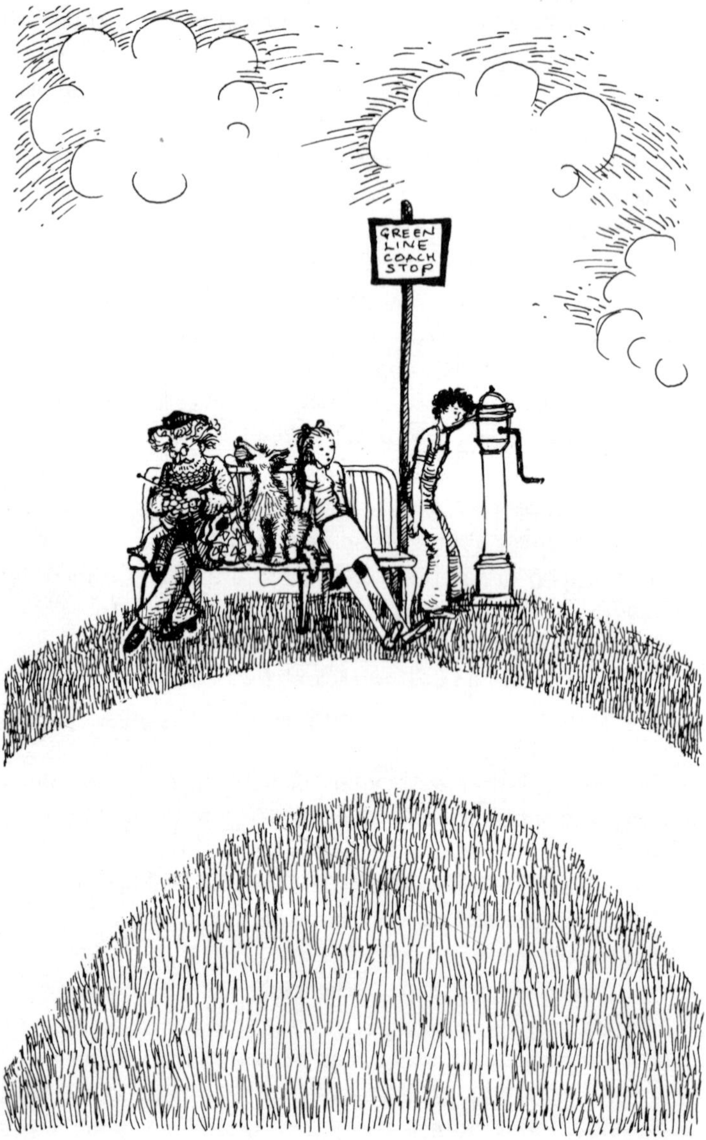
GREEN
LINE
COACH
STOP

bench, and on the bench was Jane's grandfather, knitting. Alexei was beside him, chewing the ball of wool.

"Good grief!" said Maria.

"Good heavens!" said Jane's grandfather.

"Woofle!" said Alexei, with his mouth full.

Jane was so exhausted that she could not think of anything to say at all. She had a long drink of water from the pump and then sat down beside Alexei on the bench. Maria pushed him off, and joined her.

"Well, well," said her grandfather, pleased. "Here we all are, to meet Miss Smith. Does anybody by any chance know how to pick up dropped stitches?"

"No," said Jane and Maria, together. "But I'm very good at dropping them," said Maria.

"A pity," said Jane's grandfather, shaking his head. "I am knitting Miss Smith a woolly hat, and it may not be ready before her arrival. Here comes the coach."

Jane looked out over the countryside. A long and winding road led down the other side of the hill and out through the fields into the far distance. At the very end of it, almost at the horizon, a small green coach was moving towards them.

"I have nothing else to give her," said Jane's grandfather, knitting faster. "I thought of roses, but they're too expensive. Then I thought of making everything tidy — she likes things tidy — but my back hurt, picking up all the bits. Then I thought of painting her house white — white is our favourite colour — but by that time, I was due to come and meet the coach."

"I shouldn't bother about the knitting," said Jane. "Look down the hill."

He looked, and dropped thirty stitches in one go. "Do my spectacles need changing," he enquired, "or is Kenilwood somewhat different?"

"White," said Jane. "Your favourite colour," she reminded him. "The whole town is white and tidy and smelling of roses."

"How nice," he said. "At least, I suppose so," he added, doubtfully.

Jane gave him a brief description of what had been happening since half-past four that morning. "It sounds," he said, "rather inconvenient."

"Very," agreed Maria. "Especially for people with favourite handkerchiefs."

"But I expect everything will come back," he went on hopefully.

"You tell us," said Maria.

"The most worrying thing," said Jane," is Mr. Smyrnovitch."

"Ah, yes, Pompous. He passed me on the road about half an hour ago. I thought at the time he looked rather worn."

"Worn?" cried Maria. "I should think he was practically dead."

Jane's grandfather picked up his knitting again. "No doubt things will sort themselves out," he said.

There was a loud rumble and a bang, and the coach began to ascend the hill, groaning on its wheels. "Here it comes!" exclaimed Jane's grandfather, getting all excited. The coach slowly dragged itself to the top. Alexei was on his feet, barking. The door slid open.

The first person to come down the steps was Mr. Smyrnovitch. "Good morning, Alexei," he said. Jane's grandfather ignored him, being occupied with welcoming the next person. So Mr. Smyrnovitch had to address himself to Jane and Maria. "I ran out of paper," he said, in an injured tone. ("Thank goodness," thought Jane.) "I then mounted this coach," he continued, "and met Alexandra. It struck me as most odd that she should be aboard, since I was unaware that she ever travelled at all. She informs me that she has been learning to keep house from our mutual sister, who has given her a very extravagant wedding present of fifty pounds. Not that I approve of anything to do with the matter — however, she paid my fare, so I don't complain." And he jogged off down the road, to find the Kenilwood Running Club.

"It's lovely to see you," said the old lady, shyly. "What a beautiful smell."

Jane's grandfather presented the woolly hat, which he had more or less finished.

"A lacy tea cosy!" she cried. "Just what I need."

They set off down the hill, Jane's grandfather carrying the suitcase. "The town looks different, somehow," said the old lady. "Oh!" she said, in distress. "Where are all the birds?"

Jane looked at the sky and the trees and the surrounding countryside. It was quite true that there were no birds anywhere.

"Do you think," she said, slowly, "that birds might be counted as untidy things?"

"Surely not," said the old lady, rather startled. Jane's grandfather looked uncomfortable.

"It may well be time," he said, "that I stopped Thinking."

They explained the situation to the old lady, who agreed that perhaps he had better stop. "It seems a pity," she added, regretfully, "to get rid of that very nice rose smell. But on the whole I think I prefer the town its normal colour: and a little dirt is sometimes healthy. And birds," she said, "are necessary."

"Quite true!" cried Jane's grandfather. "I will now stop Thinking."

They walked on for a few minutes. Nothing changed at all.

"I forgot," he said sadly, "how difficult it is to stop."

"What you need," recommended Maria, "is a lemon sorbet."

He shuddered.

"I've gone off it."

Miss Smith went slightly pink around the ears, and coughed. "If I might make a suggestion," she said hesitatingly, "a row on the lake would be very pleasant. I seem to remember that once before it was helpful."

Jane's grandfather immediately said that this would be a very good idea. Maria thought so, too.

"Alexei loves rows on the lake," she cried. "He adores being in a crowded boat, with someone rowing really fast. I don't suppose two of his friends could come as well?"

"Another time," said Jane's grandfather, firmly. "Miss Smith needs to be quiet after her journey."

Jane decided that probably her grandfather also needed some quiet. Day and night for all that week, he had been pacing and tidying, and since at least two o'clock in the morning he had been climbing hills and waiting for coaches. "We'll go ahead of you," she said, "and get Miss Smith's house ready."

Miss Smith gave them the key, and they ran off down the white and shining road.

They stopped at Jane's house on the way, to pick a bunch of flowers from the garden. Most of the furniture turned out to be in the garden as well. Jane's mother was washing and scouring and scrubbing inside. "This is the most confusing house-cleaning I've ever done," she announced. "Every time you take your hand off the floor cloth, it disappears. Sweeping the floor is easy, though — there's nothing to sweep. I expect," she said resignedly, "that it is all connected with your grandfather."

"Everything will be back to normal, soon," said Jane reassuringly. She made inner calculations, and decided that her grandfather and Miss Smith should just about have got into the boat and pushed out into the lake. However, half an hour later, when Maria and she had unpacked Miss Smith's suitcase and filled her house with flowers and opened all the windows, the situation was still as before. Out in the street, most people were looking very angry indeed, and glancing suspiciously at anyone who passed by, as if it was all their fault. The milkman had given up even trying to put milk down, and was handing it out direct from his van.

Jane and Maria had lunch and then went back to the park. It took three-quarters of an hour more to get there, and still nothing changed. The park was so clean and litter-free that it looked almost artificial. Out on the lake, Jane's grandfather had shipped the oars, and he and Miss Smith were enjoying the sun. Jane and Maria jumped up and down on the shore and shouted; Alexei, getting excited, swam out to the boat and circled round it, barking. Eventually, it came in to shore, stopping on the way to pick up Alexei, who had forgotten to reserve enough strength to get him back.

"Delightful," said Jane's grandfather, wobbling slightly as he made fast the boat. "Lovely," agreed Miss Smith, wobbling even more as she climbed over the edge. "But still no birds," she said sadly. Alexei's legs collapsed altogether, and Maria had to get in and help him out.

"You haven't stopped Thinking," accused Jane.

Her grandfather turned huffy. "I've done everything I can," he said. "It's not my fault if my thoughts for what Miss Smith wants are stronger than water."

"But Miss Smith doesn't want it."

"You tell my thoughts that."

They set off towards the gates in silence. The Park Keeper, with no litter to occupy him, was lying underneath a tree, soaking up the sun. "I expect this is something to do with you, sir?" he enquired, opening one eye.

"Yes!" said Jane's grandfather, snappily.

"Well, what I say is," said the Park Keeper, closing his eye again, "it's a bit of all right. A good idea."

"Just what I say!" agreed Jane's grandfather. Jane and Maria looked at each other in despair. He began to walk faster, with a smug and self-righteous expression, but had to slow down his steps because of Miss Smith.

They were now out on the pavement. Miss Smith's steps became heavier.

"Miss Smith," said Jane's grandfather solicitously. "You are tired. You are all baggy under the eyes."

"Just a slight headache," murmured Miss Smith. They walked on a few paces. Jane's grandfather stopped again.

"There is something wrong," he said.

Miss Smith wiped away a tear that had rolled to the end of her nose. "I don't mean to complain," she said apologetically, "but it feels so very strange having no birds in the park."

"Well, well," said Jane's grandfather guiltily. "I expect they will come back. Well, well," he repeated several times to himself on the way back, looking doubtful and uncertain.

Eventually, they reached Miss Smith's house. The hedge was empty and birdless. Miss Smith suppressed a sob.

"Your case is unpacked," said Jane anxiously.

"We've opened all the windows," added Maria. "There are flowers in the vases."

"How lovely," said Miss Smith, choking with tears.

"Well, well," said Jane's grandfather, again. A long silence followed, while Miss Smith took out her handkerchief and quietly dabbed at her eyes. Then, suddenly, very high up in the sky and a long way off, a tiny grey speck appeared. Nobody saw it except Jane. It was joined by another, and yet another, until the whole sky was full of them. "Look!" she said.

"Birds!" cried Miss Smith. She had hardly called out before they were flapping and swooping about her head, and making themselves at home in the hedge.

"I must go and find that special loaf of bread," said Miss Smith, excitedly. "My sister baked it particularly for them, with little shreds of fish for the seagulls."

Jane and Maria stayed outside to watch the street turning grey and ordinary. All around, people were rubbing their eyes yet again, and trying to understand what was going on. Most of them finally gave the whole matter up for lost, and returned indoors. "They should wait," said Maria. "Imagine all the bits and pieces there are to appear."

Nothing appeared, however, but dust. Maria was most disappointed. "I did think I would get Seraphina Andrews back," she said dolefully.

Jane had her eyes shut. There was something at the back of her mind that was trying to come to the front. Up on the hill, they had looked at the town, and everything had been white except the trees and the grass and the people. And something else ...

"Maria!" she said, suddenly. "What's very big, and all different colours, and out beyond the main road and the gasworks?"

"Is it a riddle?" demanded Maria. "There's nothing beyond

the gasworks. Except," she said, slowly, "for the rubbish dump."

They reached the rubbish dump in three minutes. "My goodness glorious gracious!" exclaimed Maria. "I didn't know there were so many things in Kenilwood to begin with."

The dump was mountain-high. Toffee papers jostled rings and bracelets; feathers and flower-petals covered handkerchiefs, balls, beads, coins, carrots and crayons. Seraphina Andrews was right on top of the nearest heap, with Maria's mother's wedding ring folded neatly inside her. And far into the distance stretched rows of milk bottles, looking white and nourishing, mounds of letters, looking secretive and interesting, and piles of newspapers, looking out-of-date.

"We could stay here for days and days!" cried Maria. "Drinking all the milk, and reading all the letters!"

Jane's conscience got the better of her, as usual. "I think," she said, "that everyone else should know about it before it gets dark. Supposing all the cats had to do without milk — or supposing someone had their heating cut off because they hadn't read their Final Warning letter?"

"The news is out, anyway," said Maria regretfully. "Here comes the Kenilwood Running Club."

The Kenilwood Running Club jogged around the corner and screeched to a halt. Then they leant on each other's shoulders, while they caught their breath. "Here, gentlemen," announced Mr. Smyrnovitch, pouncing on a pile of white paper and letting it trickle triumphantly through his fingers, "is our paper chase. Now, who dare say that I cheated?" He unfolded his bag from his pocket, and began very carefully to ladle the bits of paper back inside. Most of the Running Club, being of a rather more sensible turn of mind, directed their energies to organisation, and set off in couples to spread the news through the town. Maria's great-uncles stayed behind to drink milk.

Meanwhile, the sky was turning pink and violet behind the rubbish dump. Jane and Maria collected their letters and newspapers and various belongings, including two jumpers, all Alexei's balls for the previous year or two and all Maria's handkerchiefs, with assorted initials, and went home.

CHAPTER FIVE
Changes

One Sunday lunch-time, a month after the town turning white and the rubbish disappearing, Jane decided to tell her mother about the marriage.

"Mother . . ." she said, drawing a pattern on the tablecloth with her finger, "Grandfather is going to get married."

There was a long silence. Jane looked up from her pattern, and found that her mother was also doodling on the cloth.

"Mother . . ." she repeated, in a louder voice. Her mother jumped violently, making all the cutlery rattle. Her eyes came into focus.

"I was thinking about your grandfather," she said apologetically. "Did you say something?"

"Mother," said Jane patiently, "Grandfather . . ."

"A very nice dinner," announced her father, bustling in and dumping his tray on the table. "I should like another tray for tea, if you please, and chocolate buns . . . A special visitor will be arriving to see me."

"Who?"

"Ah," he answered, going mysteriously out again.

"Far too many people around here," said Jane's mother severely, "have far too many secrets. First, that parrot. Where is he spending his week-ends? Second, your father. Why is he suddenly working so hard on his Ancient Egyptians, and who are these unexplained visitors? And third — a very strong third — your grandfather."

"Mother . . ." said Jane. She was interrupted by a muffled crash.

"If I didn't know better," said her mother, "I would say that crash came from inside the wall." She rose to her feet, and put her ear to the wall. Several more subdued bangs echoed out of it. "Very strange!" she said.

Jane tipped her chair, and considered what to do next. It seemed to her that whenever she tried to make herself heard, something immediately burst out to prevent her. She made one more attempt.

"Mother . . ." The parrot flew in at the top of the window, landed on the water jug, and upset it all over the table. Jane went to her room, took out her writing-paper, wrote a long letter to her mother, sealed it up in an envelope and came downstairs with it.

The letter, however, was never delivered. All the distractions had vanished — the bangings were silent, the parrot was gone again, and Jane's father was nowhere to be seen — but something else had now started happening.

"Do you feel very hot, Jane?" asked her mother. "Do you feel very cold? Do you feel very hot again?"

"No," said Jane.

"Then this thermometer," said her mother, staring hard at the thermometer on the wall, "has turned highly inaccurate."

The red line in the thermometer was swooping up and down like a bird. "It gives me peculiar feelings," complained her mother. "I'm seasick."

There was another enormous crash, and the thermometer settled down to Fair to Moderate. "The Broom Cupboard!" exclaimed her mother, flying out of the room.

Jane's house was so very big and rambling that the back half of it was seldom used at all. It was in this half that her mother kept her broom cupboard and other untidy things. It was to the door of this broom cupboard, which was rather more like a small house in itself, that her mother ran. It was out of this door that Jane's grandfather proceeded.

"Amaryllis," he said, removing a duster from his head, "I am to be married in the spring."

"Where have you come from?" cried Jane's mother, not paying any attention.

"From my room. The spring seemed a suitable time. I have practically finished the Ancient Egyptians, and when Jane has learned to type, I will send them to a deserving Publisher..."

"How on earth did you come?"

"I came by lift," he said, pointing to the back of the broom cupboard. "Unfortunately, a little oil is needed — I came to a halt half-way and had to Think very hard, and go up and down a few times."

"I might have known it," said Jane's mother, resignedly. "The thermometer is explained."

Jane's grandfather sensed that she was slightly cross with him. "Come for a ride in the lift," he said, trying to make up.

"No, thank you very much."

"I will," said Jane, eagerly.

"Then I shall go the normal way," said her mother. "And we'll see who gets there first," she added, bitingly.

There was just room for two in the lift. Jane's grandfather swung shut the latticed iron doors, which closed with a clang and a shower of dust. "This may take a little time," he announced, pressing two buttons experimentally. One and a half seconds later, they were at the top of the house, with the doors opening of their own accord.

"I shouldn't think Mother has even started," said Jane, feeling that most of her stomach had also remained below. "But we've come to the wrong place!" she added, stepping out.

The room they were in was half dark, and extremely dusty.

It had something suspiciously like a bat hanging in one corner. "Absolutely the right place!" said her grandfather, with satisfaction.

Jane looked upwards, and saw rafters; she looked to the right, and saw another room, even worse; she looked to the left, and saw her grandfather's study.

"This house," said her grandfather, rubbing his hands, "has endless possibilities. I shall transform these three rooms into a home — Miss Smith will be enchanted."

He broke off to wave and whistle at her mother, who had just come up through the trap-door in the study and was staring around her in bewilderment. "What do you think?" he demanded.

Her mother recoiled. "It's awful," she said, not mincing words. "Shut it all off, and seal it up."

"Grandfather is going to convert it," said Jane, doubtfully.

"How?"

"First, I shall clean it," said Jane's grandfather. "Dust it and scour it and polish it. Then I shall let in the sun with four skylights, and put blue and white wallpaper up, with a pattern of roses."

"The shape is ideal," he went on. "Miss Smith loves odd-shaped rooms. The roof is flat, perfect for Miss Smith's birds. There is a magnificent view over the park — Miss Smith will enjoy it."

"One moment," interrupted Jane's mother.

"I tried to tell you," said Jane. She explained all over again, this time with her mother's full attention.

A look came over Jane's mother's face as if all sorts of things were clicking into place and making sense inside. "Now I understand," she said, "that endless knitting — those woolly hats and those jumpers and those scarves. Well, Father, I congratulate you. I shall certainly come to the wedding. I might even," she added generously, "cook the cake."

"Thank you," said Jane's grandfather, beaming. "Perhaps, in the meanwhile, you could lend me a few bottles of detergent."

Jane's mother disappeared down the trap-door again, looking rather dazed, but on the whole pleased and approving. She liked weddings. Meanwhile, to pass the time, Jane's grandfather took out his handkerchief, and began rubbing vigorously at the wall.

"I seem to remember," he said, "that there was some very pleasant violet wallpaper under here." Layer after layer of ingrained filth fell away, and eventually a small spot of violet began to glow through. "There seems to be rather more dirt," said Jane's grandfather, disconcerted, "than I had calculated for."

"Never mind," said Jane cheeringly. "Just think how much bigger the room will be when all the dirt has gone. Unless," she thought to herself, "it's only the dirt that's holding the walls together."

Her grandfather's face had turned vague and musing. "How well those clean and tidy thoughts worked last time," he remembered.

"I don't think you'd better," said Jane.

"And I," said her mother, stepping out of the lift, "absolutely forbid it. What fun this lift is," she went on. "It even goes down beyond the Broom Cupboard if you jump up and down hard enough — I discovered a cellar stocked to the top with bottles of elderflower champagne that I'd entirely forgotten. They'll come in useful for the wedding reception."

"You and Jane, Amaryllis," said Jane's grandfather, graciously, "may begin to clean the walls, while I move my History of the World to a safer position in the sitting-room. A lifetime of work," he added, hurrying away, "is in that History. And all my fortunes. It would not do for it to get damp."

"Poor Father," said Jane's mother, applying herself busily to the wall. "He lives in a world of his own. No one would publish that History in a thousand years." After ten minutes' hard elbow-work and half a bottle of detergent, she had only succeeded in uncovering three square inches. "This room doesn't need washing," she said. "It needs a hammer and chisel."

Jane's grandfather had to make three forays across the room to pile all his History onto the floor of the lift: he then breathed in hard and squeezed himself round beside it. The lift went down, groaning heavily. Meanwhile, Jane's mother finished the bottle of detergent and gave up. "Let's see what it's like on the roof," she said.

Jane skinned her nose on the chimney as she came into the open, and she bumped her shoulder on the trap-door, and she kicked her mother, who was coming up the step-ladder behind. But when they had both finally sorted themselves out, and were standing on the flat roof, their aches vanished.

The view was glorious: the whole of the park, and the lake, and the river lay spread out beneath them like a painting in green, blue and gold. Where the park finished the countryside began, and faded into the horizon in a haze of purple.

A very angry banging sound came up from below, and the roof shuddered. "Whoops!" cried Jane's mother, grabbing hold of the chimney.

Jane got on her knees, to see what was happening. Two trap-doors down, her grandfather was wrestling with an enormous carved wooden chair, far too big to come through the hole. "He can have that chair, and welcome," said Jane's mother, peering through beside her. "It came all the way from Russia — in fact, I think it was his grandfather who carved it. But he'll have to chop it into little bits before he ever gets it up into the room."

Jane's grandfather lost his temper and began banging again: the roof shuddered dangerously. "A great deal of all this," said her mother, darkly, "seems to me to be not a very good idea. This roof needs a professional builder."

"Miss Smith has fifty pounds that her sister gave her," said Jane. Her mother made a noise somewhere between a laugh and a cough. "Fifty pounds," she said, "might pay for one skylight-window. Five hundred would be more like it. Ugh!" she went on.

"Pardon?" said Jane.

"Ugh!" repeated her mother. "Something nasty is happening! This roof has swallowed my foot!"

Jane leant forward to see, but was put off balance by the chimney bending suddenly sideways. Her ankles gave way, and she fell to the roof, and bounced. "The roof's gone springy!" she cried.

The roof had suddenly turned into a trampoline, soft and rubbery. "Don't bounce too hard, Jane," recommended her mother, pulling her foot out with a pop. "I would hate you to bounce over the edge."

Two seagulls landed on the gutter, and rebounded into the air. Jane attempted a somersault, but landed on her back, in which position she continued to move gently up and down, watching the sky sway above her.

"Father!" called Jane's mother, through the trap-door. There was a guilty pause.

"You called?"

"What are you doing?"

"Moving furniture, my dear Amaryllis."

"What are you thinking of?"

"Moving furniture."

"Not about roofs becoming soft?"

"No, indeed!"

Jane's mother sat down to consider. After a while, she said: "That furniture — exactly how are you moving it?"

"Never mind how," said Jane's grandfather, sounding very uncomfortable.

"Getting warm," muttered her mother. "Saints alive!" she

cried, looking into the attic. "How did that chair come up?" She let herself down by the ladder, bouncing on every rung. Jane heard their voices floating up to her through the rubber, bubbly and elongated as if they were coming through water.

"This chair," said her mother accusingly, "has gone bendy."

"When one has useful thoughts," replied her grandfather, "it is ridiculous not to put them into practice. The chair came through the trap-door most beautifully."

"You are irresponsible, Father."

"I am not."

"You are. The whole place has turned flexible. Now stop Thinking, at once."

"I have stopped Thinking."

"I have not. The back of your mind is still full of highly squidgy thinks — thoughts," she corrected herself. "What you need is a nice lemon sorbet."

"He doesn't like it any longer," called Jane.

"That was when Maria was going to make it," called back her grandfather. "As your mother makes it, with slivers of crystallised lemon on the top, things might be different."

"Jane," cried her mother, "go down into the kitchen and fetch me the ingredients. I shall stay here, against further disaster."

Jane bounced down the step-ladder, along the floorboards and into the lift. It was exceedingly rubbery: the gates sprang open and shut five times. In the broom cupboard, things were much firmer. As she walked along the downstairs corridor, the floor became gradually stronger. And when she finally reached the kitchen, she found the floor, table, wall and chairs exactly as normal.

"Where is your mother?" cried her father.

"She's around," said Jane, reservedly.

"I desperately need chocolate buns," he shouted, rushing

round the room and opening drawers, "for my Important Visitor. Why isn't she here to make them for me?"

Jane collected her lemon sorbet ingredients and handed him the recipe book, open at the index. " 'C' for Chocolate or 'B' for Buns," she said.

"Where are you going?" he cried, becoming perfectly frantic.

"I'll come down soon and help you," said Jane, wondering who the Important Visitor could possibly be. Just then, she caught sight of the larder door: it was drooping. The bottom of the house was turning bendy as well. She rushed out to the lift.

The lift doors, however, would not close. They bounced into each other and bounced back, bounced in and bounced back, but close they would not. And, consequently, the lift would not move. Jane rushed through the kitchen again and out to the hall.

"Where's the chocolate?" demanded her father, despairing behind a flowery apron.

"Cocoa!" cried Jane. "Not chocolate. Cocoa and sugar." Her feet sank at least three inches into the hall floor. All the coat pegs had bent towards the ground, and the coats had fallen off. Going up the stairs was even more difficult than it had been when they were covered in cats: by the time Jane reached the bathroom, she was knee-deep in floor and could hardly move at all. She staggered to the window with her ingredients and looked out.

On the opposite side of the road, people were walking briskly as usual, carrying their shopping bags and brief-cases back and forth on a hard and wholesome pavement. Maria came out of her front door with Alexei, and waved. Alexei bounced across the road — but then, *he* always bounced. In three seconds, however, he had bounced into difficulties. His legs went out of control. They crossed, moved in different

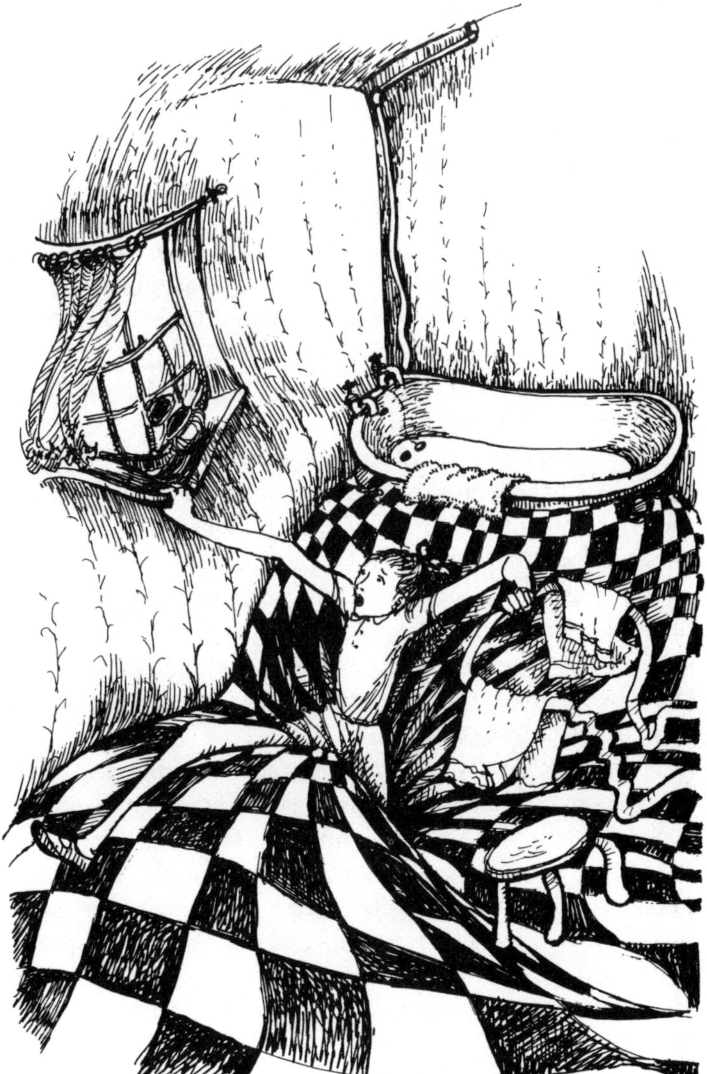

directions, and finally folded underneath him. Maria shrieked and ran: half-way there, she also started to bounce.

Jane began to rush down to help her; then she changed her mind and began to rush upstairs with the lemons; then she realised that it was no use trying to rush anywhere. She was stuck.

The bathroom floor got deeper and more gloopy. Jane collapsed into it, pulled herself up and sank steadily down again. She put one hand on the window, which bulged outwards, another on the towel-rail, which went into a squodge. Meanwhile, she heard Maria and Alexei arriving through the side door. Voices came bubbling up to her.

"Maria, my dear child," said Jane's father, "do you know how to make chocolate buns?"

"Not in the least," said Maria. "But Alexei knows how to eat them. Bring them into the sitting-room when they're ready — the poor dog needs to lie down quietly. Where's Jane's grandfather? I want to speak to him."

Jane was up to her waist: she had never imagined that a bathroom floor could be so stretchy. Just as she sank past the level of the window-sill, she saw a very dignified man being taken by surprise directly beneath, and falling across the pavement in a painful-looking position.

Then there was a tremendous, rubbery bang, and everything sprang suddenly into place. Jane found herself on solid ground again, with her ears ringing. The bang died slowly away, but was followed by an ominous rumble, which grew louder and louder, ending up with a far-away crash. She ran quickly up the last flight of stairs and into the narrow passage which led to her grandfather's trap-door. And lying right underneath the trap-door, covered in dust, was her grandfather.

"No bones broken," he said, coughing out the dust. "What a good thing you taught me those exercises to do every morning. Who would have thought that my roof would collapse? It seemed such a strong and reliable sort of roof."

"Where's Mother?" demanded Jane.

Her grandfather stopped coughing, and began to look worried. "Probably still up there," he said.

Jane pulled herself hurriedly up through the trap-door. All three rooms were open to the blue sky: there was nothing left of the roof but piles of rubble and rafters. Only the great, stolid pillar of the chimney was standing squarely out against the ruins, with her mother clinging gaily to the top. She climbed down carefully, brick by brick.

"I suppose it was a bit much," she said, "to expect that poor old roof to spring back into place as easily as the rest of the house."

Jane gazed at her in admiration. "How did you get rid of Grandfather's thoughts?" she said.

"It *was* rather clever of me," admitted her mother. "I pushed him off the chimney."

Jane's grandfather's voice floated up through the trap-door. "I am perfectly all right, Amaryllis," he said. "Just in case you wondered."

"Oh, good," said her mother. "I was rather puzzled about where you could be. Well," she continued, "that puts an end to our room-converting plans. And where are you going to live from now on?"

"I suppose," said Jane's grandfather gloomily, "that Miss Smith and I will have to make do in her house. Dark and damp."

Maria met them all in the corridor downstairs, with her finger to her lips. "Alexei is resting," she whispered. "I've put the fire on for him in the sitting-room. It was a very severe shock to him. He doesn't understand," she went on, giving Jane's grandfather a nasty look, "when people let their thoughts get out of control."

"The fire?" shrieked Jane's grandfather. "I put my History

of the World in that room. It could go up in flames at any moment. Why, if it was even faintly singed, it would be a disaster."

"Oh, that's what all that paper was," said Maria. "I used a big wodge of it to prop up a leg."

"A dog's leg?" demanded Jane's grandfather, turning pale. "Propped up by my History?"

"No, no," said Maria reassuringly. "A strange man's leg."

The man in the sitting-room was the one Jane had glimpsed out of the bathroom window. He was no longer resting his leg on the History of the World, but reading it, instead: and his face was interested and excited. "This is superb!" he announced.

Jane's grandfather stopped in his tracks, and his eyes began to shine. "Oh, I wouldn't say it was as good as all that," he said, modestly. "After all, I have not quite finished writing it, yet."

"The section on the Ancient Egyptians," went on the man, "is particularly strong. We will certainly publish it."

"Pardon?"

"Are you surprised?" said the man. "After all, you invited me here to look at it."

"Did I?" said Jane's grandfather, puzzled.

"I can promise you at least a thousand pounds in advance."

"What?"

"We have not had a good History of the World for fifty years. In fact, I think the Ancient Egyptians could be even longer. Would you have time to go to Egypt to do further research? Expenses paid, of course, and you may take a Personal Assistant."

"A thousand pounds?" repeated Jane's grandfather. "To rebuild my attics with?"

"To do anything at all," said the publisher, taking out a contract.

Jane's father burst in at the door. "Listen to me, Amaryllis!" he cried. "When you are cooking chocolate buns..."

"Alfred!" interrupted Jane's mother, looking rather stunned. "This gentleman..."

Jane's father spotted the Publisher. "My Important Visitor!" he gasped, rushing out.

"Who was that?" demanded the Publisher.

"Just my son-in-law," said Jane's grandfather, in an off-hand manner. "He also has written a History of the World. Very inferior."

Jane found her father's History on the mantelpiece, in a smart blue folder. "This appears to be the one I came to examine," said the Publisher, leafing through it. "But it seems a bit boring."

"Just what I've always said," agreed Jane's grandfather triumphantly. Her mother slipped out to the kitchen, to break the news.

By the time Jane's father came in, the contract was drawn up and signed. He was white in the face, and his nose looked long and sad. "I'm sorry," said the Publisher.

"It doesn't matter," said Jane's father heroically. He put his tray of chocolate buns down on the table, and Alexei leant forward and swallowed the lot. Jane's father gave a despairing squeak.

Even her grandfather began to be upset. "You could draw the pictures," he offered, uncertainly.

"No," said her father. "But it was a very kind offer." The telephone rang, and he dragged himself out of the room to answer it.

Jane, Jane's mother, Jane's grandfather, Maria, Alexei and the Publisher sat in unhappy silence. Everything seemed to have turned sour. The sun went behind a cloud.

Jane's father suddenly reappeared in the doorway, cheery and joyful. His shoulders were thrown back proudly. "I have just been appointed," he cried, "the new Foreign Correspondent for the *Kenilwood Herald*!"

"Good man!" cried Jane's mother. "Does this mean another safari?"

"The first story I shall be covering," he said, proudly, "after one or two week-end trips to America to interview the President, will be on the Future of the African Hippopotamus. And they agreed right away that I could take my wife and daughter with me."

Jane looked up at the sky, and saw that the sun had come out from behind its cloud. Her grandfather and the Publisher were now arguing about how much more he should write about the Ancient Egyptians. Her mother and father took out the atlas and began happily drawing ship-journeys.

"Come on, then," said Maria, taking the short cut out of the window. "Let's go and exercise Alexei's leg in the park. On the way, we'll buy a box of chocolates, and your grandfather can pay me back later."

"Pay you back?"

"Of course," said Maria. "It was all due to me. If I'd never put his History under the Publisher's leg, none of this would have happened."

"But if Grandfather hadn't made the pavement go bendy, then the Publisher's ankle would never have twisted, and it wouldn't have happened either."

"Well, he can have the Turkish Delights, then."

They picked a bunch of flowers out of the window-box as they went, and dropped them in to Miss Smith on the way to the park, with a note to tell her that Grandfather was now rich, and she would probably be going to Egypt as his Personal Assistant.

CHAPTER SIX
Strange Places

Jane was just about to get out of bed one morning when an envelope slid under her door. It was pink and white, with a pattern of silver bells around the edge. She leant over from where she was lying, picked it up and found a small card inside. The card began "You are invited to the wedding . . ." Her grandfather had finally decided on the date. Jane leapt out of bed and rushed into the next room, where he was staying until the roof was put back on again.

"Congratulations!" she cried.

"Thank you," said her grandfather, looking sad and miserable.

"Is something wrong?" said Jane. "I thought you wanted to get married."

"Naturally, I want to," he replied, "and very quickly, so that my Egyptian trip can be a honeymoon too. No, no, nothing at all is wrong."

He began tapping nervously on the wall — and then, seeing her watching, he put his hands behind his back —

And then he sighed

— and then pretended the sigh had been a yawn.

Finally, he gave up. "I'm worried about my map," he said.

"What map?" said Jane.

"Exactly," agreed her grandfather. "I've lost it. I had it twenty years ago, but now it's gone. And it is the only one in the world," he added, "that shows the way to the secret tomb of Rameses II, which I especially want to visit, and explains all the inside bits when you get there. And I must, must," he cried, desperately, "find it before we sail."

"I'll help you look for it," said Jane.

So they looked. They looked in cupboards and behind chairs and in the tops of wardrobes. They took all the earth out of window-boxes and looked underneath and they shook the mats and they even pulled up the carpets. There was nothing at all.

"There is one room left," said Jane's grandfather doubtfully. "At the back, next to the broom cupboard. I used to sleep there when I first came to Kenilwood from Russia. In fact, it was the only room that existed. The rest of the house was sort of built up around it."

They hurried down the stairs and through the kitchen to the back of the house. "Don't go in!" shouted Jane's mother, putting the hoover in the broom cupboard. "The Park Keeper is asleep on the bed."

"What?" said Jane's grandfather. "In my special room?"

"Yes, and you have only yourself to blame. Who was it that made the pavement go bendy outside the house? Well, then. He rode his bike over it, and the bike crashed, and the wheel buckled, and his home is too far away from the park to walk every morning, so he has to stay here until the bike is mended. And it will take at least three weeks."

"Tchah!" said Jane's grandfather.

"And Tchah to you!" replied her mother. "You ought to be ashamed of yourself. He was feeling miserable even before you did anything, because he's not making enough money from the boating lake to buy bulbs for the flowerbeds. You just made things worse. He hurt his toe as well, so it will be a long walk for him, even from this house. In fact, I think you should apologise."

"I'm sorry!" shouted Jane's grandfather, through the key-hole.

"Not now!" whispered her mother furiously. But it was too late — the Park Keeper had already woken up.

"Good morning, everyone," he said, putting on his cap. "Eleven o'clock — I should have been at the park two hours ago. Excuse me if I rush."

"Perhaps you should get out of your pyjamas, first," said Jane's mother. "Anyway, why not let the park take care of itself, for a while? Stay here and rest."

"Yes, do," said Jane's grandfather, kindly. "You can help me look for my map."

The Park Keeper's eyes went all sparkly and interested. "Maps!" he said. "I love maps! But no, no," he went on, turning away with regret. "It is my duty to care for my park."

By the time he was dressed and full of breakfast, however, he had changed his mind again. "Bill the grass-cutter will have opened up the gates," he said. "So I'll just stay for half an hour. Well, maybe three quarters. I was always good at finding things."

They searched thoroughly through his room, behind the curtains and the chair covers, in the fireplace, and even under the floorboards, but with no results. The Park Keeper looked anxiously at his watch. "Half-past eleven," he said.

But Jane's grandfather had had another idea. "Down in the cellar!" he cried.

"Don't be silly," said her mother. "The cellar is full to the brim with bottles of elderflower champagne. There's not a crack that a map could slip into, between them."

"Aha," he said. "But there is another cellar, below that." He pushed the bed to one side, revealing a large trap-door and a spiral staircase, disappearing into darkness. Jane's mother sighed, but she collected four torches from the broom cupboard and handed them round. Grandfather took a candle, instead.

"This is a useful trick I learnt while tomb-exploring," he said. "When the candle goes out, you know there isn't any air."

"I should think you would know that beforehand," said Jane's mother. "You would be dead."

Jane's grandfather became very huffy and annoyed, and refused to talk any more, and ignored her when she told him to wrap up warm. "Well, you are being nasty this morning," said Jane's mother. But Jane could tell that he was simply getting more and more worried in case his map was lost for ever.

Jane went cautiously down the spiral staircase behind everyone else. It made ominous creaks all the way, and they had to jump the last two steps, which had disappeared completely. Now they were in a vast grey room with mouldy walls, beneath the elderflower cellar. "I can't think why you need to go to Egypt to do research," said her mother, shivering so much that her torch rattled. "You have a ready-made tomb right here."

Jane trailed her finger along the wall and dust showered down. There was nothing apart from dust, however: certainly no map, and no hidden places where a map could possibly be.

"Time to go!" said Jane's mother eagerly.

"No, no," said Grandfather. "One more cellar."

"What?"

"A very small one," he said, opening another trap-door. An even colder breath of air swept up from it, and he began to shiver too. "I wish we had central heating down here," he said, reproachfully.

"I didn't know there was a Down Here to put central heating in," said her mother. "And I told you to bring a coat in the first place." She was getting snappish and bossy. "You're cold," she said, "I'm cold, Jane's ears are blue, and Mr. Beechmast wants to get to his park. Why have your eyes gone funny?" she broke off.

Jane's grandfather's eyes slowly un-glazed. "Oh, dear;" thought Jane to herself. "He looked rather Thoughtful."

So she was not altogether surprised when, a few moments later, she began to feel warm and cosy. "How lovely," said her mother, stretching luxuriously.

"Now, perhaps," said Jane's grandfather, "you'll stop complaining. It's very difficult," he went on, "to Think things warm in a cellar. All the heat rises upwards. So I hope you appreciate it."

"Oh, yes, I appreciate it very much," said Jane's mother, as they went down the second spiral staircase. "The only thing that makes me slightly uneasy," she said, "is wondering where all that extra heat is rising to."

The walls of the second cellar were green and drippy: Jane kept her fingers well away from them. She shone her torch into every chink and cranny, but nothing appeared. "It's terribly hot," said her mother, flapping her hand in front of her face.

"Some people," replied Jane's grandfather, "are never satisfied." He wiped his forehead with a handkerchief and the Park Keeper took off his coat and hat. Jane felt her ears turning from blue to red.

"Stop Thinking now, Father," said Jane's mother.

He looked at the cellar wall, and coughed. "He can't, as usual," thought Jane.

The cellar was getting hotter and hotter. "Right!" said Jane's mother. "That's enough of this nonsense. Back upstairs. It's time you had one of my lemon sorbets: time also for Mr. Beechmast to go to the park."

"Thank you!" said Mr. Beechmast gratefully. He ran up the spiral stairs ahead of everyone else, and then slid down again, gasping like a fish. Jane propped him up, and fanned him.

"Mr. Beechmast!" cried her mother. "What's wrong?"

"It's HOT!" said Mr. Beechmast. "The higher you go, the

hotter it gets. It's absolutely impossible," he added, "to climb up into the house again."

"Now look what you've done," said Jane's mother severely to Grandfather. "You make me very cross."

Jane took off her jumper, wondering how her grandfather could be brought to stop thinking, when there was no way of reaching the lemon sorbet ingredients. The heat was terrible.

"How fortunate it is," said her grandfather, opening another trap-door, "that these cellars carry on underneath."

The next cellar was slightly cooler, but did not remain so for long. And it was just as empty as the other two. "Where on earth is that map?" muttered her grandfather.

"I do hope the park is all right," chimed in the Park Keeper dolefully.

"In my opinion," said Jane's mother, "you should all stop worrying about maps and parks. Frankly, they won't make much difference when all of us are suffocated and unconscious."

Soon the heat was again so bad that Jane's grandfather had to open yet another trap-door. As they went down the next flight of steps, Jane heard something rather unexpected. It was a gurgling, splashing sound, very soft but quite distinct.

"Did you hear a gurgle?" demanded her mother.

"Did you hear a splash?" cried the Park Keeper.

Jane's grandfather slapped himself on the forehead. "My underground river!" he exclaimed. "Well, well, and to think that I'd forgotten all about it."

The spiral stairs broadened out, and then suddenly turned into a rope ladder. "And my special ladder!" said Jane's grandfather. "How it all comes back to me. It took three weeks to make this, back in 1918."

Jane's mother leapt back onto the spiral stairs. "You made this ladder?"

"It is a perfectly good ladder, Amaryllis," said Jane's grandfather stiffly. "Someone checked the knots for me."

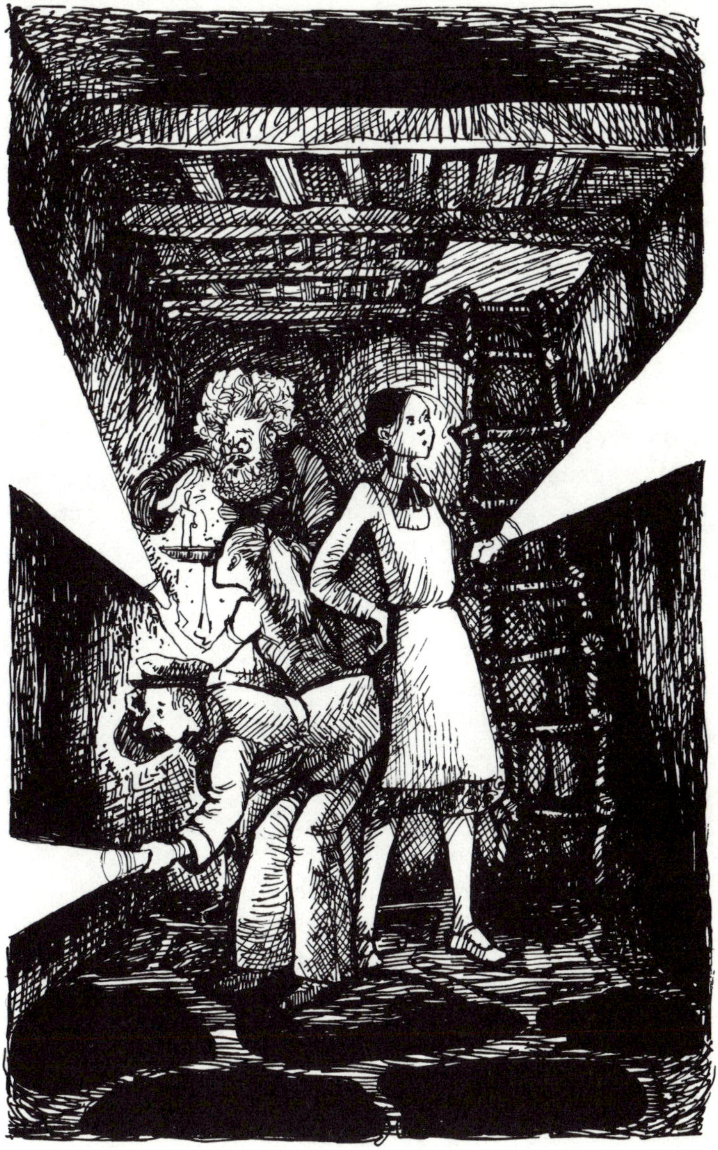

The ladder swung violently from side to side as they climbed down, but they were soon on solid ground again. Rocks and pebbles crunched under Jane's feet: she was standing by the side of a deep and narrow river. Her mother shone a torch across the water. "Where does this river come from?" she demanded, in amazement. "And where does it go?"

"The answer to both questions," replied Jane's grandfather, "is 'I can't quite remember at the moment, but no doubt it will come to me in time'. The Blue Danube!" he cried.

"I'm sure it's not the Danube," said her mother.

"No, no," he said, holding the candle up. "The *Blue Danube* is my boat." The light flickered on a long, thin, wooden boat, propped up on a smooth and sloping piece of rock at the side of the river.

Jane's grandfather untied the boat and it slid down into the river. "She's still seaworthy!" he announced, jumping up and down inside. "Come for a punt!"

"No," said Jane's mother.

"It's very cool on the water."

Jane's mother wavered.

"You'll come, won't you, Jane?" said her grandfather, picking up the punting-pole. Jane could not resist it. She climbed into the boat.

"Oh, very well then," said her mother, getting in too. The Park Keeper pushed the boat off and leapt in behind her. It moved off downstream, carried along slowly by the current. Jane's grandfather hardly had to push at all with his pole.

"Thank goodness!" said her mother. "I feel cooler already. What a bit of luck, finding an underground river — we can always jump in and bathe, if your thoughts get too hot."

"My thoughts are not here," replied Grandfather. "I left them behind on the shore." Jane explained about the effect water usually had on him, and her mother gave a sigh of relief.

"So everything will start cooling. But too late to save the house, I expect," she said gloomily.

The river widened, and the cave roof shot up again into the darkness. All around them, water swirled in black eddies and washes, and slapped at the bottom of the boat with hollow booming noises. Jane trailed her hand over the side, and felt a fish touch it lightly in passing. "This is one better than Kenilwood Boating Lake!" cried her grandfather.

"Shush!" said her mother. "Remember whom we have in the boat with us."

"No need to whisper," said the Park Keeper cheerfully. "I think it *is* Kenilwood Boating Lake."

Jane and her mother looked at each other by the light of their torches. "There, there," said her mother, soothingly. "This has been a very difficult time for all of us, Mr. Beechmast. When we get out, you must have another nice rest."

"I've always wondered where the lake came from," he went on, not paying any attention. "The thought of a whole underground river never occurred to me."

Jane's mother shone her torch up at the roof of the cave in an absent-minded manner, and gasped. "Stop!" she cried, grabbing Jane's grandfather by the knee. He collapsed, luckily into the boat and not out of it. "Really, Amaryllis!" he said, annoyed. "It's obvious you have not the faintest idea of how to behave in boats. Rule One — never grab your boatman's leg. If I had not very cleverly remembered to hold onto the punting-pole..."

"Father," interrupted Jane's mother, "be quiet for one moment, and look above you."

Jane shone her torch up in the same direction as her mother's and it lit up an amazing sight. Long icicle shapes shone down at them, in glorious shades of pink, blue and green. "Looks like we've sailed into the Arabian Nights," said the Park Keeper, in a hushed undertone.

"Stalactites!" whispered Jane's mother. "They must have been growing here for thousands of years." Her voice echoed faintly out across the water. The boat was in the middle of a vast, calm pool: Jane could see the passage-way they had just come from, but the sides of the cave were too far away for the torch-light to catch. The reflections of the stalactites shimmered in the water all around them.

"Oh, yes," said Jane's grandfather airily. "I remember now — the stalactite-thingummyjigs. Quite pretty. Well, time to be moving on," he said impatiently, brandishing the punting-pole.

"Be careful!" hissed Jane's mother.

"There's no need to worry," he said. "I used to pass them a hundred times a day, back at the beginning of the century, and none of them ever fell off."

Soon, he had punted them out of the cave and into shallower waters. The walls began to close in on each side. "Seems a pity," said the Park Keeper, regretfully, "that there were only us to see them."

"It should be just about here," interrupted Jane's grandfather, peering into the darkness, "that we stop." The boat crashed suddenly into a jutting-out rock, and Jane found herself mixed up with everyone else. When she had sorted herself out, she looked up and saw light directly above. "Just as it used to be," said her grandfather, with satisfaction. He secured the boat on the piece of rock, caught hold of the bottom of another rope ladder, and hauled himself towards the light. The water rushed darkly past the boat and poured down into a narrow tunnel, hung over with more stalactites. The Park Keeper shone his torch at them and whistled under his breath.

As Jane climbed the ladder, she heard a faint clatter of wings above her head and the sound of a grass-cutter mowing a long way off. Then her head was in the open air, and she was blinking in the sun. She had come out in the middle of a hollow tree.

"Just by the boating lake!" exclaimed the Park Keeper,

coming up behind her. "I was right. How handy! And to think I've passed this tree a hundred times, and never suspected anything at all."

They let themselves down onto the grass by the sticking-out branches. "I like punting much better than walking," said the Park Keeper. "In fact, if Mr. Bostov will let me, I'll punt back and forth to the park every day while I'm staying at your house."

"If there's any house left to stay at," said Jane's mother sadly.

Jane wandered down to the side of the lake and found Maria kneeling there. "Oh, good," said Maria, when she heard about the underground river. "Alexei would love punting in the dark. He needs a comforting treat, after this nasty shock."

Alexei was sitting in the lake, looking miserable and harassed. With one hand, Maria was holding firmly onto his collar, while with the other she soaped and scrubbed and untangled his coat. He was blowing bubbles through his nose.

"Just hang on a few more minutes, my noble dog," said Maria comfortingly. "It will all be over, soon." She shook the last half-bottle of shampoo over him, and rubbed it up into a green froth. "You would never believe," she whispered to Jane, as she rinsed him and put him on the lead, "the things I've been finding. Fourteen mouldy acorns he's been carrying around with him since last Autumn."

Alexei shivered and dripped. "I think you ought to take him somewhere warm," said Jane.

"I am," agreed Maria. "Your house. It will still be a very good radiator."

"We can't go by boat," said Jane. "Unless Alexei knows how to climb ropeladders."

"No," said Maria regretfully. "Never mind, I'll knot one up this evening and give him some practice."

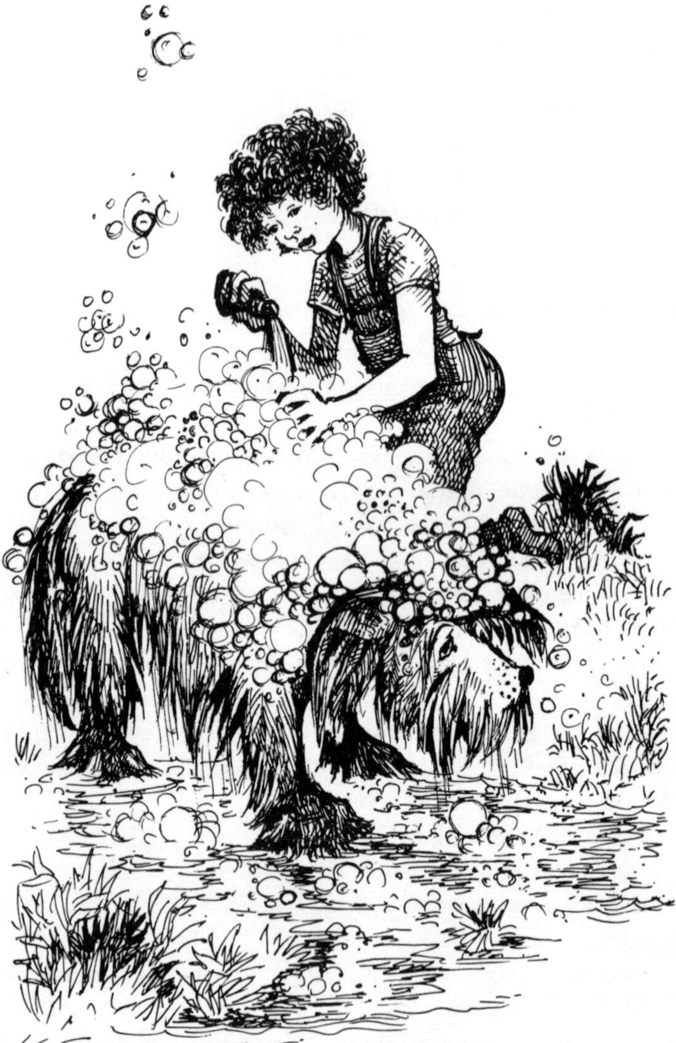

Half-way to the gates, they passed the Park Keeper, who was hammering an orange notice into the hollow tree. "Your mother has just had a wonderful idea!" he cried, beaming. "Boat trips to see the stalactites, at ten pence a ride! I should be able to buy three thousand daffodil bulbs by September!"

A long queue was already forming. "We're going home," said Jane to her mother, who was holding the notice steady.

"You're braver than I am," said her mother. "The house will probably be cracked into little pieces. Except for the chimney — we do have a nice, strong chimney."

Just outside the park gates, another thought occurred to Jane, and she ran back.

"Where's Grandfather?"

"He returned by boat," replied her mother. "I asked his permission about the tourist trips and he seemed not to mind. He said he didn't care about anything any more. In my opinion," she added, standing back from the notice to make sure it was straight, "he should never have raised his hopes so high about that silly map. Anyway, if there was anything left in the house, it would have been... Whoops!" she cried, suddenly remembering something. "We left your father inside it!"

"He'll be all right," said Jane. "He went to America."

"Not another of those week-end trips for the *Kenilwood Herald*?" demanded her mother. She shaded her eyes and looked at the sky. "That's probably his aeroplane coming back now, then. Let's hope it doesn't pass directly over what was once our house."

Jane ran back to Maria, and found her hopping up and down impatiently. "Alexei is a quarter dry already," she said, "and I must say, he's coming out most peculiar."

Before they went round the corner into Jane's road, they looked at Alexei again, and he was astonishing. Not only was he dry, but shining and brilliant: his hair stood out in a two-foot halo all around him, glistening in the sun. "I feel as if I'm walking an utterly unknown dog," said Maria. "Five minutes in your house will dry him off completely and give him the finishing touches."

They turned the corner and bumped into Jane's grandfather, who was doing a little jig on the pavement. "Glory, Hallelujah!" he sang. "I've found my map, and everything is charming! What a lovely afternoon! What a fetching dog — he can come to my wedding. I always hoped you would change the other one."

"Where did you find the map?" asked Jane.

"My thoughts found it for me," he replied proudly. "The heat peeled all the paintings away from their frames, and it dropped out from behind the Mona Lisa. My thoughts," he said contentedly, "always turn out useful in the end."

"Well..." said Jane, doubtfully.

"The Bendy thoughts weren't very useful," said Maria. "Apart from catching that Publisher for you. What use is a fallen-in roof?"

"In this case," he said, with triumph, "lots of use. None of the heat got trapped in the house — it simply went straight out through the hole in the top. So you have me to thank that the house is still standing.

"Anyway," he went on, before they could say anything, "my map is found, which is the main thing. And that Park Keeper person will have enough money for his daffodil bulbs — the flowers should be out just in time for my wedding. And I happen to know," he said, finishing off his jig with a flourish, "that, for those of us who are feeling empty inside, Miss Smith is even now cooking Baked Almond Slices for tea."

CHAPTER SEVEN
The Exact Opposite

"Now, then, Jane," said Jane's mother, waving the cake knife, "you can have up to three slices of cake, with a seasickness tablet between each slice." She cut the cake, and her hat blew off into the dark and sloppy water by the pier, where lots of little fishes swam up and nibbled it.

All the family, which now included Miss Smith, and two guests, Pompous and the Park Keeper, were having a combined wedding reception and birthday party on the pier; and the elderflower champagne had made them all very pink in the nose.

Jane's father carefully removed the icing from his slice of cake, wrapped it in his paper napkin and handed it to Jane's grandfather. "Please accept," he said, politely, "this trifling icing."

"Thank you," said her grandfather. "It makes up for the icing you stole from me at Amaryllis' wedding. And I shall not say any more rude things about you.

"I don't really like icing, anyway," he added, looking slightly ashamed — but he ate it.

The two ships lined up by the pier blew their horns, the clouds blew across the sky, and Maria and Alexei blew onto the landing-stage. "Just in time for the cake!" said Maria. Alexei took four slices, without pausing to say anything.

Maria pulled Jane to one side. "Happy Birthday," she whispered. "I think Alexei is going to be sick."

"Oh, no!" said Jane.

"He was sick before we set out," went on Maria, "he was sick on the bus, he was sick on the train, and he was sick behind that bollard three minutes ago. I can't understand it — I keep giving him Strengthening Glucose, but it doesn't seem to help at all. What might possibly work," she said, "is seasickness tablets."

"I have some," said Jane.

"Thank you," said Maria, taking them. "You can have this bottle of Strengthening Glucose in exchange. Drink it quickly — ten days on the sea to Equatorial Africa is no joke. What horrible stuff sea is," she added, looking distastefully at it. "All large and wet. It was much better on television."

Jane tipped up the bottle and drank. "It tasted very strange," she said. "I feel sick, too."

"Don't be silly — you're not even on the ship yet."

"I feel worse and worse."

"A dreadful thought," said Maria, with her hand to her mouth. "The Strengthening Glucose could possibly have gone off."

"On board!" cried Jane's father, picking up three suitcases and the parrot cage and rushing up the gangway into the ship for Equatorial Africa. Jane's grandfather and Miss Smith kissed everyone, including Alexei, and went up the next gangplank, to the Egyptian ship.

The Egyptian ship pulled away first. "Goodbye!" cried Jane's mother, waving her handkerchief, and remembering just too late that she had been saving her wedding-cake icing inside it. "Don't forget to bring us back a bit of pyramid!"

"Goodbye!" cried Jane's grandfather and Miss Smith, sharing a handkerchief.

"Goodbye!" shouted Jane's father, taking farewell photographs. "I wish to goodness those ducks and seagulls would get out of the way," he muttered. "Still, I suppose that wherever Miss Smith — I mean Mrs. Bostov — goes, birds go too."

Even as he said it, the Egyptian ship was too far away for photographs. Jane's mother looked at her in surprise. "You never waved, Jane — and why are you looking at your feet?" But Jane was feeling too sick to answer.

The African ship blew its horn, the waves blew in and crashed against the pier, and Maria and Alexei blew from the landing-stage to the top part of the quay. "Good luck!" shouted Maria, as she went. Pompous and the Park Keeper shared the last bottle of wine, and wept sentimentally.

Soon the ship for Equatorial Africa was chugging steadily out of the harbour into the open sea. "How one does go up and down," observed Jane's mother. "What a good thing that we all took those sea-sickness tablets."

"Looks like a storm blowing up," said one of the sailors. "Funny, that — the forecast said Fair and Calm." The sky turned purple, and the waves began to swell and boom. Jane leant over the rail and moaned gently to herself. "I wish Grandfather was here," she thought. "Perhaps he'd be able to Think me cured." But her grandfather's ship was already a dot on the horizon, with hundreds of tiny dots flying round it.

Rain started to sweep across the deck, and the wind tugged and flapped at the loose deck-coverings. Jane's mother turned her around. "Jane," she said, with interest, "your face is green."

"Worst storm I remember, this near to land," said another sailor, going gloomily past. "Shush!" said his companion. "Don't scare the passengers."

Jane's mother tried to distract her with the shops selling duty-free perfume and postcards of hippos; she tried to entertain her with the desk where they changed English money for African; she tried to tell her jokes about sharks and icebergs.

Jane simply went greener and greener. Finally, her mother took her out on deck again.

"Get it over with, Jane!" she shouted, through the roaring of the waves. But Jane had never been any good at being sick. She tried hard once or twice, and then had to give up and go to the cabin. Outside the port-hole, the sky turned an angry purple, shot with forks of lightning.

Her mother came in and sat down on the opposite berth. "Jane," she said, "I have been working matters out in my mind. A horrible suspicion has come to me. I would like to think it was wrong."

"Grandfather!" said Jane.

"It is far too much of a coincidence," agreed her mother, "to be a coincidence. Your grandfather boards a ship, and immediately a most unusual storm starts blowing up. Heaven knows why he has begun thinking about storms, but somehow he must be stopped."

Jane stared at the roof of the cabin, and wondered what could possibly be done. It had been hard enough to stop her grandfather thinking before, when he had been with them, but as a small spot on the horizon, he presented a very complicated problem. "Don't worry too much, Jane," ordered her mother. "It will only make you feel sicker. Besides, I have just decided the only thing to do. I will send a telegram."

She rushed out of the cabin. Ten minutes later, she returned, rather white in the face. "They'll let me use the telegraph system," she said. "For a pound a word." She turned her purse out onto the bed. "What can I say for five pounds?"

"Two pounds will do," pointed out Jane. "Stop Thinking."

"Five pounds will be better," said her mother. "Stop Thinking Now Immediately Quick!" She wrote it out on a small scrap of paper, and went to deliver it.

"Now we await results," she announced, reappearing. The sea continued to crash up and down outside. The port-hole flew open, and flung a shower of spray into their faces. "Those waves are getting higher," said Jane's mother. "I just hope your grandfather is in a sensible mood."

"Telegram for you!" shouted a sailor, and a thick envelope landed Plonk on the bed. Jane's mother tore it open, and unfolded a vast sheet of paper. "He is the most wasteful person," she said, "I have ever known in my life."

She read the telegram aloud. "My dear Amaryllis," it said, "thank you so much for your charming telegram, received as sent, very exciting and much appreciated. Have not been Thinking in the least, hardly ever Think on water anyway, cannot understand what you are talking about. Having a wonderful time, Alexandra well and sends her regards. Love to Jane.

"P.S. It often skips a generation."

"I give it up," said Jane's mother. "The whole affair is beyond my control." She began to unpack, and put things in cupboards and drawers. At the bottom of the case was a very scrumply bundle. "My evening dress," sighed Jane's mother. "I'm supposed to be wearing it at the Captain's table. And dinner is in ten minutes' time."

Jane groaned. "Well, perhaps you had better stay here," said her mother doubtfully. "I'm sorry you'll miss seeing the Captain, in all his gold buttons." But by the time she had tried to smooth out her evening dress, and then wondered about wearing another skirt, and then finally put on her nightgown instead, with lots of lacy shawls so that no one would notice, Jane had decided that she would come after all.

"As long as I don't have to eat anything," she said.

"All right," said her mother. "But it'll be a pity, because the Captain's table always has the best food."

When they got to the dining-room, however, they found that the Captain had only invited Jane's father: her mother and she had to sit at a small table for two with a goldfish bowl in the middle. Her mother was infuriated. "Why should he have all the fun?" she cried to the man serving the food. "It's my daughter's birthday, and she's ten years old. And that empty chair at the head of the table would be quite big enough for both of us."

"That is the Captain's chair, Ma'am," said the sailor stiffly. "No one ever sits there except the Captain himself. He is in his cabin, slightly indisposed."

"Feeling sick? The Captain?"

"He is a new captain," explained the sailor. "And it is a very bad storm."

Jane's mother sat down huffily beside the goldfish, which went round and round in the bowl, goggling at her. "Poor thing," said her mother. "It looks pale: it knows there's a storm outside. I would crumble a little sea-sickness tablet into its water," she said, "but I've lost faith in those tablets, since they didn't work on you."

"It wasn't the tablets," said Jane miserably. "It was Strengthening Glucose."

When her mother had heard the story, she waved her fingers in the air and made exasperated noises. "If you had only told me before," she cried. "Maria's mother gave me the recipe for an Anti-Strengthener two years ago." She opened her handbag and uncorked a little test-tube. "It contains certain secret ingredients," she said, "not to be found in the kitchen cupboard." A cloud of nasty-smelling blue floated out across the dining-room and settled in the middle of the Captain's table. "Bother!" said Jane's mother. "Lost it. These tubes are very fiddly. Never mind, I have a spare." She uncorked another and held it under Jane's nose. "Sniff." Jane sniffed, and the second blue cloud shot up her nose.

"Better?" cried her mother eagerly. "Not yet," said Jane, with caution — but, as a matter of a fact, she did feel rather different. The room was coming into proper focus again, and her stomach was churning more slowly.

"Better?" demanded her mother, a minute later.

"Yes," said Jane. "No," she corrected, as a man went by with a plate of boiled snails.

Five minutes later, she was perfectly well. The snails went past again, and did not affect her in the slightest. "Better," she said, decisively.

Over at the Captain's table, however, things were not going quite so pleasantly. Most of the diners, including Jane's father, had pushed their snails away untouched and were looking pale and weak. The cloud of Anti-Strengthener had thinned itself out around their heads, and was taking effect.

"They look awful," said Jane. "Do you think they should take a lot of Strengthening Glucose, to cancel out the Anti?"

"Do you?" she repeated, seeing that her mother was not listening. Her mother came to herself, with a jump. "No," she said. "Let them stew. I have more important things to think about."

"What?"

"You. You and that goldfish."

Jane stared hard at the goldfish. "It looks much happier," she said.

"Exactly," agreed her mother. "And you also look much happier."

"The storm's going, at last!" cried a sailor, leaning round the door of the dining-room. "The wind has dropped and the sky is clearing."

"Jane," said her mother, "I am beginning to understand your grandfather's P.S. 'It often skips a generation'."

"I was looking at that goldfish," she continued, "while you were recovering — and it struck me very strongly that you were both recovering at the same time. Not only that, but when that man went by with his snails and you turned sick again, the goldfish dived to the bottom of the bowl and a wave splashed up against the window. You," she said, "have inherited not only my blue eyes and your father's unfortunate nose, but something rather worse from slightly further back."

"Oh, gosh!" said Jane, beginning to understand as well.

"Gosh indeed," replied her mother. "It occurs to me that if you had not made yourself sick with that Glucose, the storm would probably never have started. Your Feelings have become as dangerous as your grandfather's Thoughts."

"Anything to eat, Madam?" interrupted a sailor with a trolley.

"Thank you," said Jane's mother. "Dinner for me, and three Ship's Biscuits for my daughter. To keep your stomach settled," she said to Jane. "I can see that few things will be more vital on this journey."

Jane ate the Ship's Biscuits, trying not to remember something Maria had once told her about weevils. The people from the Captain's table staggered past them on their way to lie down. "I'm just going to check on your father," said her mother. "Stay very calm." And she walked out between the other tables and through the swing doors.

Jane concentrated on being calm, and found it boring. She dropped a few odd crumbs into the goldfish bowl; and she played with the tassels on the tablecloth; and she counted the squares on the ceiling; but after a while she began to wish very much for something more exciting. It was then that her eyes fell on a large glass of wine which her mother had been given as part of her dinner.

The light was shining through the glass and making red shadows dance on the table. Jane remembered Maria saying that wine was an extremely interesting thing to drink. Her mother returned just as she was finishing the last drop.

"Jane," she said, "you have turned completely irresponsible, and I expect you feel dreadful."

"No," said Jane, yawning.

"You don't?" cried her mother, taken aback.

"No," said Jane, half asleep.

"Then what do you feel?"

Jane made no answer — she was asleep altogether.

When she woke up, she found herself propped up against some pillows in the cabin. "Now how do you feel?" demanded her mother.

Jane tried to remember how she ought to be feeling. "Calm," she said, at last.

It was the wrong answer. "You must feel excited, Jane," cried her mother. "Excited and awake. For one and a half days," she said, "you have been too calm altogether. Asleep, in fact. The goldfish has also been asleep. The ship engines have stopped, and we have been drifting steadily eastwards.

"And perhaps I ought to tell you, Jane," she added, "that your grandfather and Miss Smith are seriously ill with the measles."

"Oh, no!" cried Jane, leaping up.

There was a sudden rumble, as the ship sprang into life. "Well done!" said her mother, looking out of the port-hole. "By the way," she went on, "don't get too calm again, but Grandfather and Miss Smith are, as far as I know, feeling fine."

Jane was very confused, but completely awake. Her stomach made a loud noise, to announce that it had also woken up.

"I'll get you something to eat," said her mother. "Remain awake, Jane, and unsick. And keep a watch for telegrams while I'm out — I found another pound note in the bottom of the suitcase, so I sent a word to your grandfather. The word was "Jane" — I expect he'll understand."

Jane lay back and wondered about the rest of her life. It seemed as if she would never be allowed to eat anything interesting or unexpected again. It was her duty to keep herself feeling normal for evermore: otherwise, storms would blow up, and ships would be wrecked, and people would drown and die. Most people had illnesses that only affected themselves, but her illnesses could wreck the world. Even worse, she thought, with a cold shiver running along her spine, she might never sleep again. Here, there were only ship engines to be affected, but back in Kenilwood there would be gasworks and traffic-lights and kidney machines in hospitals. She began to get panicky, and immediately heard the waves hitting harder against the outside of the ship.

Another brown envelope flew in at the door and landed at her feet. "Telegram!" cried a sailor. Jane tore it open.

"Dear Amaryllis," ran the telegram, "and Jane, if you happen to be there as well — thank you very much for your latest telegram, even if you did forget to apologise. We are still having a charming honeymoon, although the ducks have their eyes closed and the engines have stopped. Has Jane by any chance fallen asleep? The nice man sending these telegrams for me turns out to be the Park Keeper's son, so he lets me send them at a halfpenny a word. Love and kisses.

"P.S. It may well be that Jane is the Exact Opposite."

Jane handed the telegram to her mother, who had just come in with some ordinary, reliable food: bread and butter and a glass of unfizzy lemonade.

"The Exact Opposite of what?" said her mother. "What on earth does he mean?" She held the telegram up to the light, looked at it upside down, and finally threw it in the bin. "He's just being silly."

Two minutes later, she took it out of the bin again, borrowed all Jane's savings and sent another telegram. This one said "What?"

Jane's grandfather's telegram came back: "I said 'The Exact Opposite'. And it generally starts at ten."

"Why will he never answer questions?" cried Jane's mother in exasperation. "Jane, tell me what this means."

Jane had already solved the last part. "It was my birthday today," she said, " — I mean, the day before yesterday.

That must be what he means by 'It generally starts at ten'."

Her mother was laughing to herself. "I'm trying to imagine your grandfather at ten years old, without the beard."

"Perhaps he would have looked like me," said Jane, dreamily.

"Not at all, Jane, you're quite different. For instance, you make things go peculiar by Feeling and he does it by Thinking. And besides, with him it doesn't work on water . . . The Exact Opposite, in fact!" she cried. "I think I've answered my own question. Well, I am clever."

"And if it doesn't work on water with him," thought Jane happily, "then it won't work on land with me. I only have to keep away from the sea, and not have too many baths, and everything will be perfectly all right."

Outside the port-hole, the sky was blue, the gulls were flying and the horizon was cloudless and bright. "Try not to remember," said Jane's mother tactlessly, "that you won't be able to go to sleep for the next eight days. I wonder if it works in a canoe? We're travelling by canoe all the way into the centre of Equatorial Africa."

Jane hoped it would not, but felt deep inside her that it probably would. In her mind's eye, she saw the canoe overturning, typhoons arriving, crocodiles launching themselves through the water . . .

At this point, a dark cloud actually appeared outside the port-hole, and Jane's mother told her to stop it at once, and go and explore the ship. "Just keep feeling interested and happy, Jane," she said, and Jane went out, trying hard.

The ship had four decks, each as long as a small street and at least as wide. Jane ran all along the top deck and back without stopping, but by the time she had finished, her legs were collapsing and the ship was making ominous coughs and splutters. To help herself think calmly, she took a soothing look over the side of the rail, and watched the water creaming and curving beneath.

It is a mistake to stare at moving water for too long: sometimes it makes your head go strange inside. Jane turned away and blinked her eyes to get back to normal.

"Was I imagining it," said a very fat lady, going past on a very thin gentleman's arm, "or did the ship just go round in a complete circle?"

"I shall speak to the Captain," said the very thin gentleman. "Things like this are just not meant to happen on an ocean-going cruiser."

Jane went down to the second deck, and found herself in the dining-room again. The goldfish was looking dizzy. She went down to the third deck, and walked past rows of cabins, and people sitting on fold-up chairs, and table-tennis games and swimming-pools and life-buoys. Then she tried to go down to the fourth deck, but found herself on steps going sideways. The steps stopped at a small passage-way, which led to another set of stairs, which should have led, according to Jane's calculations, back to the third deck, but instead ended up somewhere quite different. There were more rows of cabins, but these were all empty, and the wind was sweeping in and out of their doors and making them whistle. Jane walked on, hoping to come across something recognisable, and then she walked back, trying to find the stairs again. And then she realised that she was lost.

Half an hour later, she was beginning to think that she was probably lost for ever. "There's no way out!" she thought desperately. A cloud of spray splashed onto the deck, and beyond the rail white horses began to appear on the waves. Jane forced herself to be calm.

Far off in the distance, she could see her grandfather's ship, with the dots of birds around it. In three days' time, they would be opposite the Straits of Gibraltar, and after that, the ships would divide off into their separate routes. "And then," thought Jane, "I won't see Grandfather again for at least two

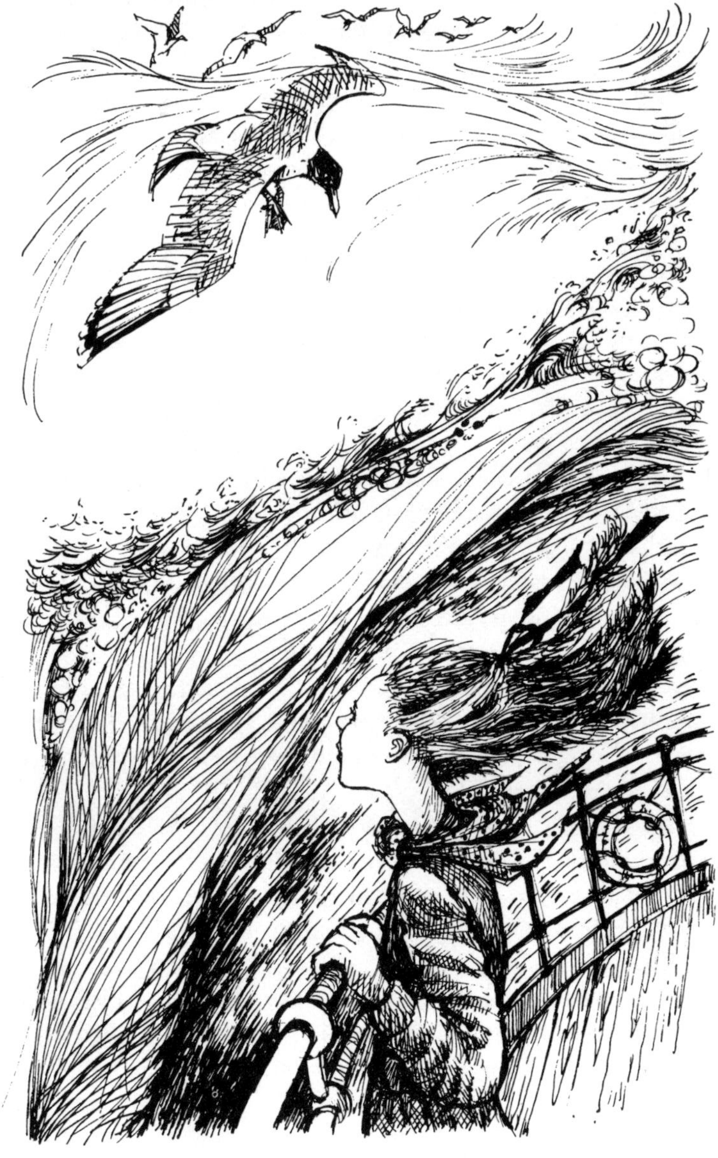

months — if I ever see him again at all. I'll probably have sunk the canoe to the bottom of the Equatorial African River by then."

"I don't know what to do," she said sadly to a passing seagull. "And neither does Mother. And Father would have no idea. Grandfather is the only one who could possibly help, and he's three quarters of a mile away — I couldn't reach him even if I jumped into the sea and swam. And I would probably drown on the way. And then the goldfish would die too, and perhaps the ship would sink."

Up in the sky, two enormous grey clouds moved rapidly towards each other. "If only they were our ships," thought Jane. "If only the ships were coming together, instead of sailing apart."

Suddenly, the water started to lift and swirl. Far out across the sea, the waves seemed to dip towards a dark centre. "A whirlpool!" she thought. "And we're on the edge of it!" A few moments later, she realised that the other ship was caught on the further edge, and that, very gradually, they were being pulled in together to the centre. Jane felt a burst of joy inside her: but then she remembered what happened to ships in the middle of whirlpools. The sea would suck them down and batter them to pieces. She would never even have time to reach her grandfather.

She tried desperately to make it stop. "It's my feelings that are doing this!" she said to herself. "It's my wanting to be with Grandfather." But the more she tried to feel that the ships should be moving apart, the harder the whirlpool sucked. The engines of the ship roared and choked, as it tried to escape — but the water roared louder than they did, and pulled more strongly. Steadily, it tugged both ships towards the centre.

Jane felt as if she were frozen to the rail — she could not think, speak or move. The wind whistled around her, and plucked at her clothes. She shut her eyes.

All of a sudden, everything was absolutely quiet. The wind had dropped, the whirlpool had disappeared and the sea was as flat as a table. Even the engines were quite silent. Two gulls plumped down beside her on the rail as she opened her eyes.

The other ship was a hundred yards away, floating peacefully, with its decks grey and deserted. Then people began to appear from below and run to the side, waving and shouting. A man with a loud-speaker climbed up onto one of the lifeboats and his voice boomed across the water.

"Request Permission," he cried, "to meet you for immediate consultation!"

Somewhere in Jane's ship, another voice replied. "We are sending a boat!" it said. "Please be ready to receive us!"

Music floated over the water — someone had struck up a tune on an accordion and people were dancing and waving coloured handkerchiefs in the air. The two gulls flew from ship to ship, and finally settled on Jane's shoulders: one of them had a note in its beak.

"Remember to bring a shady hat," said the note. "Alexandra says she would love to have you — and anyway, Egypt is a much more intelligent place to visit than Equatorial Africa."

While Jane was still staring at it in surprise, a blown tarpaulin moved to one side a few yards away, and her father emerged from a hidden flight of stairs.

"All your things are packed, Jane," he said. "Are you ready to go?

"Your mother," he went on, "thinks, heaven knows why, that this storm has something to do with you. It's best to humour her. Some sort of telegram arrived from out of the blue and immediately she began insisting that you go over and stay with your grandfather from now on. Here's the telegram, if you can make head or tail of it."

He fished a scrumpled piece of paper from his pocket. It

said "Opposites Sometimes Cancel Each Other Out. Bring also bird seed, if possible."

Jane pondered the telegram, and decided that her grandfather was probably right. "But do I need cancelling any more?" she said. "The storm has gone."

"I don't pretend," said her father, "to know what anybody is talking about. However, one thing I do know — the storm has not gone."

Jane looked up at the sky and down at the sea. Nothing was moving. "And now," said her father, "look out into the distance."

Out beyond both the ships, and the wide circle of calm which enclosed them, the storm still raged and the waves still crashed up and down in the wind. "Naturally, the Captain won't tell us what is happening," said her father ominously, "but I know something about hurricanes. We are in the Eye. All hurricanes are calm in the middle, but outside, they are nasty. So, if there is really anything in what your mother is saying, I suggest we get you to your grandfather as soon as possible, before the Eye moves on."

They reached the next deck just as a boat full of official-looking sailors was being lowered into the water.

"Stand Clear, all passengers!" said one of the sailors impatiently.

"I am no ordinary passenger," said Jane's father, with impressive dignity, "I am the Naval Correspondent of the *Kenilwood Herald*. The Captain has given me special permission to cover the event. With my secretary, of course."

"She's a very small secretary," said the sailor, peering hard at Jane.

"That's why I chose her: to take up less room."

The sailor grumbled to himself, but at last he said that he supposed it would be all right.

"Thank you," said Jane's father. "And perhaps I ought to

mention," he added, indicating Jane's suitcase, "that wherever I and my secretary go, my documents go too."

"Here, now!" said all the sailors together. But luckily, they were distracted by a far-away boom from the hurricane, and somehow Jane and her case and her father and most of the sailors managed to squeeze in together without anyone actually falling overboard.

The sea in the Eye of the hurricane was clear and calm. Shoals of little fishes were moving just underneath the surface, and beneath them layers of larger fish, some with whiskers and thin, filmy tails. They were so thickly packed together that they could hardly move out of the way in time for the boat to go through. If anyone had dipped in a net, it would have come out full and wriggling.

"It's the Eye," said one of the sailors. "All the fish for a good fourteen miles must be swimming around under here." He looked at the grey storm raging outside the circle, and shivered. "We'll be in trouble," he added, "when she moves on. Though somehow," he said, looking through his binoculars, "if I didn't know Hurricane Electra better, I'd say she was thinning out."

Jane glanced back at the ship they had left behind them and saw a bright red hat and a waving hand on the fourth deck. "Your mother told me," said her father, "to tell you and your grandfather to keep a good watch on each other."

The sun flashed on something metallic that her mother was holding in one hand: it was a bird-cage. Fifteen seconds later, the parrot was cleaning its wing-feathers on Jane's shoulder.

Now they were almost half-way to the other ship. "She *is* thinning out!" said the sailor, still peering at the hurricane. "I'd never have believed it."

The dance on the other ship began to move faster, as people flung their knees up in the air and clapped in time to the music. Some of the coloured handkerchiefs drifted down towards the boat, as one sailor switched off the motor and two more rowed them to the bottom of a long rope-ladder. "That's the weirdest thing I've ever seen in my life," said the sailor, polishing his binoculars, as if something was wrong with them. "She's gone!"

The first person Jane saw when she reached the top of the ship was her grandfather, with a sunburnt nose and his beard at least a foot shorter. "I decided to cut off the knitted bit," he explained, seeing her trying not to stare. "It was hot. Well, Jane, welcome to the S.S. *Ruritania* for the next two weeks!"

"What?" said the sailors who had brought them on the boat.

"She's my secretary," said Jane's grandfather, thinking he was cunning. The chief sailor opened his mouth to object, but was distracted just in time by a floating red handkerchief, and joined the dance instead.

"How pleasant to be together, Jane," said her grandfather, "cancelling each other out. Did you by any chance bring a packet of bird seed?"

"No," said Jane. "I brought another bird." The parrot flapped its wings and transferred itself to her grandfather's shoulder. "No bread-roll again at supper tonight," he said sadly. "Never mind, I expect Alexandra will be pleased."

A large and sombre man in gold buttons appeared beside them. "Ah, Captain Goshle!" said Jane's grandfather, cheering up. "Jane, let me introduce you. Captain Goshle is writing a History of the World. Once we get to Egypt, he's going to skip ship and do some research with us."

"Shush!" said Captain Goshle anxiously.

"Oh, yes, I forgot: we are keeping it quiet. Can you ride a camel, Jane?" said her grandfather. "I'd better telegraph Egypt to book another."

Captain Goshle and Jane watched him wandering absent-mindedly through the dance. "I admire your grandfather," said Captain Goshle. "So many old people just shut themselves away in attics and forget about the world."

"Sometimes, they come out," said Jane.

"Let me take a photograph of you, Captain," interrupted Jane's father, clicking busily with his camera. "A close-up on the gold buttons, please. Now, have you any comment to make on the situation?"

"Well, not really," said Captain Goshle vaguely. "It all seems to have turned out quite nicely. The engines are working again, and the hurricane doesn't appear to be there, and, actually, we might as well be on our way."

"In that case," said Jane's father, "I will say goodbye to my daughter. Jane," he went on, handing her the camera, "this is my second-best camera. I want you to take lots of pictures of anything interesting — not too many of your grandfather. In particular, the pyramids, from all four sides. I've decided I'm too good for the *Kenilwood Herald,* so I'm setting up a little newspaper of my own. Pictures, advertisements, articles!" he cried, as he went down the rope-ladder. "And every week a new chapter from my History of the World." The boat pulled away from the side of the ship. "You can be the Egyptian Correspondent!" shouted her father. "And Miss Smith, or Mrs. Bostov, or whoever she is, can do Bird Articles."

Jane took a photograph of the dancing, and then an interesting idea came to her. As well as being a photographer, she could write. Seven long inside-stories, giving true explanations of all the peculiar things that had happened to her in Kenilwood, and out, since she was nine years old. She would begin with the cats — and then go on to the meteor in the park — and the free samples — and the discovery of the underground river — and the litter that had strangely disappeared — and the roof that had oddly collapsed — and perhaps even the hurricane and the whirlpool. But on second thoughts, the decided that probably no one would believe a word, so instead she went to find her grandfather.